MANAYUNK

MANAYUNK

Wealth becomes the elephant in the
room for five friends from Philly.

John Gelhard

ISBN-13: 978-0692166284 (Custom Universal)
ISBN-10: 0692166289

Printed in the United States of America

Interior Design: Ghislain Viau

To Mom and Alexis

PROLOGUE

"WHAT ARE YOU DOING HERE ALREADY?" Chuck asked me as he was entering the conference room where our weekly meetings were held.

"Just thought I'd get here early and work on some things while I waited for the meeting to get started," I replied. But really I wanted to sit dead center of the conference room table, facing the glass wall that separated the room from the hallway.

"That's where I normally sit."

"Well, there's plenty of room left. I'm sure you can find another spot that's to your liking," I replied.

Chuck and I were still working things out between the two of us. I was the new sales engineer, a position he'd been working in for the last two years. Nothing serious but there had been a few instances during my short tenure when Chuck felt I was overstepping my bounds or getting in his way. Just before I arrived, Chuck was the only sales engineer on the team so everything was his. Now he had to share.

Chuck was a few years older than me, skinny, balding, serious sort of person. I could tell my existence annoyed him. He couldn't understand how I could be hired as a sales engineer with my limited experience, especially when he had to fight for the position, or how quickly I mastered the technology.

Chuck walked around to my side of the table and sat in the chair directly on my right.

"Okay. Good, keep it close. This will be the engineering section."

Eddie was the next to enter. Eddie was in outside sales and we went to college together. Eddie's and my employment rubbed some of the more experienced people wrong. We were the result of a new hiring process. Eddie and I were put through an extensive screening process that was based more on assessment than experience and work history. I scored off the charts in the engineering evaluation and Eddie did very well in the sales screening. Rick and Chuck represented the old guard. Those guys were hired for entry level positions and then had to work their way up through the ranks. They were "internals", also known as "bellheads" (the term was derived from Ma Bell's logo) and Eddie and I were "externals". Internals were more likely to be union members and leftovers from the time when the phone company operated as a monopoly. Management felt internals were coddled, spoiled employees. Externals were brought in as the new blood. Internals understood that things operated a certain way inside the phone company and didn't question the system. Externals saw things differently; they were more likely to push back and look for ways to improve the system.

"What are you guys doing here so early?" Eddie asked.

"What's it to you?" Chuck shot back.

"Just that you guys are taking up some prime real estate. I like to sit over there just in case some hottie from sales support happens to saunter by."

"Well, at least you're using the time well. You wouldn't want to be paying attention to what Sherry had to say or anything like that," Chuck preached.

"I can multitask," Eddie replied. Then he walked around the other end of the table and sat directly to my left.

"This is going to look weird," Chuck observed.

"Well, I'm not moving. I was sitting here first," I responded.

"Either am I. No way I can make it through one of these meetings without at least the possibility of seeing some babe walk by."

Rick entered the room. Rick was a Senior Account Manager. That just meant he had been there longer than some of the other sales reps and the company was trying to appease him. *Bigger title, smaller raise.*

"Hey guys. Why are you'll sitting on the same side of the table?" Rick asked.

"Hey Rick. Declan was sitting in my usual seat, so I had to sit here and Eddie wants to be able to check out the women that walk by," Chuck explained.

"That's why I like to sit over there," Rick said, "and there's no way I'm looking at your ugly mugs all meeting long," Rick sat down next to Chuck.

Rick was a very polished and deliberate sort of salesperson. He was well dressed and formal. He was as equally annoyed by Eddie as Chuck was with me.

Just then, John, the lead installation tech walked in. John was an ex-marine. He was older than the rest of us and a no nonsense kind of guy. John would be the best representation of an internal.

Installation techs ruled the old phone company. They made the most money and could do just about anything they wanted with virtual impunity. They were hard and fast union guys. The phone company operated in a certain manner and that wasn't to be questioned. If these guys couldn't make it to a customer location, too bad. Let the customer call in and reschedule. What else were they going to do, go to the *other* phone company? Dispatch and the techs could make a sales rep's life a nightmare. A sales rep would sell a service and work within the company's less than customer friendly scheduling windows - eight to noon, noon to five, or even worse, eight to five - and hope for the best. If a tech got a hair up his or her ass and decided that he or she wasn't up for a job, that person would simply "no access" the customer. That meant the tech was dispatched but couldn't locate the customer. Nevermind the fact that these were business customers and the installations were scheduled during normal business hours. It would turn into a "he said, she said" situation where the tech, not the customer, was always right. The phone company had a bizarre way of managing the outcome. Since the customer was already pissed, there was nothing much that could be done to make them un-pissed, so why piss off another customer that hadn't been pissed off yet? So dispatch would reschedule the missed the jobs the same way new jobs were scheduled, on a first come, first served basis. The missed customer would go to the back of the line. It was up to the sales rep to placate the customer. Subsequently, there was a lot of bad blood between the techs and the sales people.

"Hey ladies," John started. "How sweet. You guys getting ready for a foursome? Should I come back?"

"Very funny," Chuck replied. "When I came in, Declan was sitting in my seat."

"You have assigned seating in this department?" John asked.

"No, but people should respect tradition," Chuck replied.

Sherry, the sales manager, was next to enter. "Oh, good. You guys are getting chummy. That's nice to see. I knew you guys could work out your differences."

"They're actually fighting over center court," John informed her.

"Oh jeez. I need you guys to work together. We can't run a cohesive, productive department if you're all at each other's throats."

It was 2003. Along with Sherry, Eddie, Chuck, Rick and me, there were five other sales reps that made up our team in the large business department at the phone company. We all met every Monday morning to discuss company direction and matters at hand. That morning, Sherry asked John to attend.

Our office was located in a high rise in downtown Philadelphia. We all had to wear badges to get past security and up to our floor. If you forgot your badge, you had to call up and have someone come down and sign you in. It didn't matter that you passed the same security people every day. For all they knew, you were canned the day before and looking to settle a score. But with the badges and the locked doors, you'd think we were a diamond wholesaler.

Our conference room was a dingy space, retrofitted inside the suite. It had no exposure to the outside world. Outside, the sun moved across the sky. Inside, the artificial light remained constant; without a clock and knowledge of the outside world, the room's visitors would have no idea of the time of day or year. The coffee stained carpet stretched across the floor had been compressed to the point that it provided as much cushion as would a thin blanket. A wall of glass separated the room from the hallway that let people passing by know that there was a meeting in session and they might not want to scratch their asses or grab their nutsacks. Unless of course, it was a meeting your buddy was attending and he was the only one looking. I liked to sit so I could see out into the hallway.

The conference room table was one of those midsized oval shaped deals covered in phony wood laminate to hide its shitty pressboard interior. There were holes towards the center for electrical and AV cords and coasters strewed about. Directly in the center was a good sized conference room phone. One wall was mostly whiteboard. On the shorter wall, hung a flat screen TV. The chairs that surrounded the table, were the high backed, fake leather variety and fifty percent more chair than anyone needed.

Sherry sat at one end of the table. John sat at the other end. Then there was the Eddie, me, Chuck and Rick bundle, sitting in the center. The rest in attendance were scattered around the room. The late arrivals had to use a notebook to write on because there was no available table space. Actually, there was but the damn chairs were so big there wasn't enough room to fit them all.

On the whiteboard, there were remnants of a hundred previous meetings. It was a rainbow of dry erase marker colors. Then there were the dry erasers that looked very similar to the chalk erasers from grade school. Apparently, eraser technology had not advanced at the same rate of speed as other technologies.

You could tell a lot about the people in attendance by their choice of stimulant. Eddie was drinking Dunkin Donuts coffee; Chuck and John were drinking breakroom coffee; Sherry was drinking tea; Rick was drinking a Big Gulp; I had Starbucks.

Another variable was the choice of attire. Sherry was wearing a tight top (all her tops were tight) and some pants with vertical stripes. Rick was wearing a suit. Eddie wore a shirt and tie. Chuck, John and

I took advantage of our tech titles and the possibility of needing to enter a hard to reach phone closet or demarcation point to wear polo shirts and jeans.

Sherry was one of those women that men found either incredibly sexy or not attractive. Eddie thought she was one of the sexiest women he had ever seen. I, on the other hand, thought she could lose a few and didn't find her face all that pleasing. Chuck was in agreement with Eddie. "Come on, her tits are massive and she has the sexiest voice ever. I have to remind myself to look up constantly," was Chuck's assessment.

"I'd do anything to fuck her. I keep trying to find out of town opportunities so we'll need to travel together," was Eddie's.

Sherry did have a sexy voice, I'll give her that, and she was an asset to bring on most appointments. She was going to appeal to at least one of the males in attendance but she wasn't a threat to the women. She did have massive breasts but they were in proportion to the rest of her body. She also had a weak chin and lifeless hair. I don't think Eddie or Chuck knew what color her hair was or that it was lifeless.

Sherry got started at the phone company right out of high school. She worked there her entire adult life. It was the only job she ever had. When she first started it was all AT&T and in full monopoly mode. Back then, people were paying ninety cents per minute for long distance and customer records were stored on microfiche. The phone company was a way for a person with limited education to enter the middle class. Up until the 2000's the phone company offered thousands of jobs that could produce a comfortable living.

The great thing about Sherry, besides her massive breasts, was that she knew someone in every department in the company that could help if you needed an override or an expedite or any other human push in a slow moving system. She was cunning; she knew exactly how to work just about any deal. I've never worked with anyone whose opinion I valued more than hers. I don't think she had any outside sales experience besides what she obtained as an outside sales manager. But outside sales people don't need to be taught how to sell - you either have those attributes or you don't - they just need someone to intervene on their behalf and help push deals through, and that was Sherry's value.

Sherry began the meeting. "Good morning everyone! Hope you all had a nice weekend."

"Good morning," everyone muttered back.

"Let's jump right in. There's a big push for new logos," Sherry explained.

New logos was a fancy way of saying new customers, not just new business. New business could be more business from an existing customer. New logos was new business from a new customer. Management had obviously sat around discussing the subject and someone came up with the term, "new logos" and the rest in attendance were either envious or excited, depending what type of team player they were.

"I've been working on some new logos. I'm real close, but it's too early to tell," one of the unnamed participants shared a piece of completely useless information. There were always a few in a group that would say what they thought their boss would like to hear.

Sherry's challenge was that the sales people in attendance were account managers, or farmers, and tended to focus on their existing customer base. They weren't big fans of hunting for new business. That would require prospecting and cold calls, activities they found distasteful. They all had gotten fat from their existing clients building out their networks for the past few years. All they had to do was show up every day and place orders. Now, that activity was slowing down.

"Does anyone have some ideas on how to secure new logos that they could share?" Sherry asked the group.

"It's always a good idea to stop by the neighboring businesses when you're visiting one of your existing customer locations," another no name suggested.

"Excellent idea! Any others?"

If you were one of the sales reps in the meeting, you wouldn't want to share too much information. If you knew a good way to secure new customers, you'd probably want to keep that information to yourself, because you were indirectly competing with the other sales reps.

"Referrals from existing customers?"

"That's another good idea. Thank you. Any others?"

"What if one of your customers changes their logo?" Eddie asked.

"Very funny, Eddie. Good to see that you're feeling more comfortable in the department. Don't get too comfortable," Sherry shot back with a smile on her face.

"Well, I'll be covering this topic in our one-on-ones, so come prepared. Next on the agenda is certifications. Declan you need to be working on that. Chuck can help you. Chuck, Declan needs to be Cisco certified, can you help him with that?"

"Sure. I have nothing better to do," Chuck replied.

"Someone's grumpy this morning," Sherry exclaimed. "Next on the list, CPE. We need to be proactively offering CPE to our customer base"

CPE stood for Customer Provided Equipment and could be a phone or computer equipment. Used to be, that the phone company wouldn't let its customers use their own phone equipment; they claimed it would contaminate the network. The acronym was created when that rule was abolished and customers started using their own devices. The term was misused in this circumstance because Sherry was referring to us selling the equipment to our customers. The appropriate acronym could be PCBE, or Phone Company Provided Equipment, but the acronym, CPE was entrenched and not going anywhere. CPE was the reason I needed to secure certifications.

"Okay, I invited John to our meeting so he could field questions. I know you all have had installer issues in the past and I thought it would be a good idea to get everything out on the table so we could move forward as a more cohesive team," Sherry announced.

John was in his late forties, stern looking and over six foot tall. He was a union man, through and through. He looked like the type of guy that wouldn't think twice about cracking the skull of some young, punk sales rep. This was a dirty trick by Sherry. She probably had her fill of our no access and missed install complaints, so she came up with the idea of inviting John. Interrogating John on the subject of technician behavior would be equivalent to questioning Quint about his shark catching abilities.

"What is it with you guys? I have customers that are sitting, waiting for their tech to show and nothing happens and then they call me. I check the order and it's been no accessed?" Leave it to Eddie to ask a question that the rest of the sales reps wanted to ask but didn't have the courage to.

Sherry lowered her head and covered her face with her hands. The rest of the group had a newfound admiration for the rookie sales rep and were all ears.

"What are you insinuating?" John asked.

"I'm insinuating that it seems like some of the installers, probably not you, have better things to do and no accessing an order is good way to knock off early." Eddie replied.

"Okay, okay, this wasn't supposed to be an inquisition. John, Eddie here is new and doesn't know any better. What's something the sales people could do to avoid having their customer's installations missed? Any suggestions?"

"Don't make promises that can't be kept. That's one idea." John replied.

John was referring to a salesperson offering a more narrow window for arrival than was available. For instance, in some circumstances the installation time would be set for anytime between eight and five. If a customer objected to the wide interval, a sales rep might promise that the tech would arrive "in the morning" or "late afternoon" or would call before going and hope for the best.

"You know, this isn't going the way I had hoped. How about you all send me some specific examples of installation related issues and I will discuss those with John and get back to you? Does that work for everyone?" Sherry placated.

There was mumbled acceptance from the group. John made it evident that Eddie might want to watch his step around the office.

"Oh, almost forgot, we received a RFP from the Royal movie theater chain. They're bidding out their network," Sherry proclaimed.

RFP stands for Request for Proposal or Request for Pricing. It's a formal request for pricing from all the invited participants. It's not a popular sales opportunity due to the amount of competition and work required for submission.

"I heard AT&T is entrenched," Rick offered.

"I heard the same thing," Chuck affirmed.

"Well, whether that's true or not my boss wants us to participate in the bid," Sherry replied.

"Give it to the new guys," Rick suggested. Rick was referring to Eddie and myself.

"You guys think you're up to it?" Sherry asked.

"Sure, why not," Eddie replied. "Declan?"

"I'm game."

"There you have it. Let's see how you guys do. The worse thing, you'll gain some valuable experience," Sherry summarized. "Okay, that's it. Good luck everyone. I hope you all have a great week. Eddie, watch your back."

Sherry's last remark broke up the group as we were leaving our seats and filing out of the conference room.

John actually admired Eddie for speaking his mind. He knew the rest would wait and bad mouth the techs in Sherry's office. Eddie, John, Rick, Chuck and I started eating lunch together and became friends. John loved to bring up that meeting and Eddie's brazenness; he thought it was hilarious. Some kid, fresh out of college, questioning the unioned techs. Eddie couldn't understand why it was a big deal.

CHAPTER 1

—◄○►—

MY NAME'S DECLAN. I HELPED CREATE MovieDate, a leading dating website and smartphone app. I was given a third stake in the company and paid a percentage of every transaction. When my partners and I sold the company to a large social networking site my net worth (on paper) totaled more than a quarter billion dollars.

I went from comfortable to incredibly wealthy in a span of less than three years. Now, I have more money than I could ever spend. It's not the level of rich where I could lose it all with a few bad investments or due to too many handouts to friends and family members. I'm floating a boat in a sea of money.

I don't think the money has changed me. I don't live on an estate or drive a sports car with scissor doors. If you met me you wouldn't know I was rich. I don't have a black Amex card or wear an expensive watch. I don't want anyone to know I have money.

I have a few friends that treat me the same way they did before I became wealthy. One friend, Chuck, cares less about money than anyone I've ever known but he has a lot to say about rich people.

Chuck believes there are four types of rich: lucky rich, self-made rich, class rich, and not rich.

Lottery winners and Google's first two HR managers are examples of lucky rich. You hear horror stories, so maybe it's not such a good thing to win the lottery but considering the odds against it, winning it has to require the greatest amount of luck. Two HR managers were amongst the first twenty Google employees. They received shares of Google stock before the company's initial public offering. One of them became an angel investor.

Do you know how rich you have to be to become an angel investor? So rich that real money becomes the Monopoly variety. Almost everything loses its value. If you're that rich, you either take up drag racing or become an angel investor. Angel investors are not betting on whether or not Amazon will show strong earnings in the fourth quarter; that's not risky enough. They're looking for businesses - can't even use the word *businesses* because it implies *profit* and *revenue* - entities that are *pre revenue* - ones that have trouble securing bank loans - *businesses* that might as well be the number twenty-two on a roulette wheel - a smile on a young man's face - the kind of investments that are subjects of financial horror stories.

Most of the time you read about the people that we're unlucky when it comes to the tech industry. Like the third founder of Apple that left the company when Jobs and Wozniak were still in the garage or the couple that spurned IBM and sent the company back to Bill Gates for its operating system. But there were a lot of regular people who just happened to be in the right place when some super genius came up with the next big thing.

Self-made rich requires a talent or skill, or an amazing desire or will. Chuck puts me in this category.

Class rich is the rich that Chuck has the least appreciation for.

Class rich grew up that way due to the efforts of a distant relative. It's a life of private schools and clubs, prestigious institutions and partnerships.

The class rich are very concerned about the not rich. To the class rich, everyone is a threat, so they attempt to insulate themselves as much as possible. But they can't protect themselves adequately with alarms and iron fences; the class rich require political policy and manipulation.

The class rich want being rich all for themselves. Their goal is to make the price of admission nearly impossible to obtain. Private school is a must. And it's not enough for your kids to have access to better schools, some push for tax breaks for the money they spend on their kids' private education, revenue that would no longer be available for public schooling.

Chuck's rich rules to live by:

Always do what's in your best interests. Make it seem like you care by creating and donating to charitable organizations, when your real goal is to reduce your tax burden.

Promote the American Dream.

Don't get Chuck started on the American Dream. He believes the rich promote that belief like the word of God. Why? Chuck believes that if some fool thinks he or she has even the smallest possibility of achieving great wealth that person will want to make sure all the advantages of being wealthy remain intact.

If you debate Chuck about this he'll ask you to explain why some barely middle class person would vote for pro rich policies and politicians?

Chuck has a list of the class rich's greatest hits. They include:

The Trickle Down Theory - The rich will help you if you help them.

Unions are Killing This Country - Workers shouldn't be paid too much or the companies they work for won't be able to compete.

You're Lucky to Have a Job - Stop bitching about working long hours for low wages and limited benefits, you're lucky to have a job. Some people are really lucky and have two jobs.

Fight for Our Freedom - Join the armed forces and risk your life to fight unjust wars that are business ventures for the extremely rich.

Weapons of Mass Destruction - In case anyone is questioning the validity of a war.

Gun control and the repeal of Roe vs. Wade. If the lower classes begin to question the distribution of wealth, make them believe that someone is trying to take their guns away or ban abortion.

Illegal Aliens - Specifically brown aliens. Ten out of ten sane people would agree that it was very wrong for Hitler to vilify the Jews. But the same ten people might jump on board if some politician did the same to Hispanics.

If you make the claim that everyone wants the same thing - a strong economy. Chuck will counter, "The class rich don't care about the state of the economy; they're never going to promote any legislation that promotes the good of the country over their own self-interests."

Why?

"The class rich look at a down economy like it's a clearance sale. They have the resources to withstand any recession. If the price of a share of stock drops or the housing market collapses, that just means they can buy more for less. And when things start to improve, they're better off than they were beforehand."

16

If you grew up not rich in Philly, it's difficult to maintain friendships with class rich people. Living in Philly is like driving an old car; you know new cars, with luxuries like Bluetooth, heated seats and climate control exist but you tell yourself you don't need that stuff. Sure the weather and roads suck, and for no good reason you have to travel to three separate stores for your groceries, beer and booze, but it's what you know. It took the Phillies over one hundred years to win a championship and maybe the Eagles will never win a Super Bowl, but nothing makes your day like the Phillies defeating the Mets or the Eagles the Cowboys. Sure all the food Philly is famous for - the cheesesteaks, Tastykakes and soft pretzels - is garbage. Then don't eat it. Who needs microbrews when Yuengling is on tap? Living in Philly is about settling. Class rich people don't like to settle.

Most of my rich acquaintances don't have any non-rich friends. They don't trust the not rich. They think they're after their money. Luckily for me, my not rich friends aren't that way.

I have two best friends, Chuck and Eddie. If it wasn't for me, there would be no Chuck and Eddie because Chuck doesn't particularly like Eddie. Eddie likes Chuck but has a funny way of showing it. Any friend of Eddie's will be subjected to ball busting and ridicule. It's Eddie's language of love. I get it, but Chuck takes it personally.

I have two other friends, Rick and John, who are more on the peripheral. All five of us used to work together at the Phone Company. I knew Eddie before that; we went to college together. I'd rather be around these guys than any rich person I ever met.

Being rich is great. Being rich and famous, not so much. But people have egos and some want everyone to know that they have money. At first, driving around in a two hundred thousand dollar automobile does the trick; but if the cute girl at Starbucks didn't see you pull up and doesn't understand how much your Audemars Piguet watch costs, where does that get you?

Personally, I like to remain anonymous. The other day, I sat outside Starbucks, completely unbothered, enjoying an iced coffee. Just then, one of the Phillies players pulled up in his nero pastello F12 Berlinetta, ran inside and came out a little later with a coffee. He was on his way back to his car when a group of people recognized him. One said "Nice walk off the other night". I guess this player drove in the winning run in a recent game. The player didn't recognize the fan or his comment, just hurried to his car and drove off. The next word out of the fan's mouth was "Asshole!"

I don't have to feign interest in something a stranger said to me or pretend to be friendly. Money has allowed me to do whatever I want, whenever I want. I don't care if someone likes me or not. If something doesn't go my way, I can jump on a plane and travel anywhere and stay for as long as I desire. I don't have to answer to anyone or anything.

CHAPTER 2

◄○►

I MET CHUCK AT DAWSON'S, A BAR in my hometown, Philadelphia. Unless you're a fan of cold, rainy, sticky, snowy weather, the fall is the best time to live in Philly. It's my favorite time of the year and Philadelphia is one of the best places to experience it. The leaves turn, the weather is brisk and it's football season.

Dawson's is a small bar located in a spot you would never place a bar if you had a desire for it to be successful. It's at the dead-end of two residential streets, ten yards from a large wall. The wall separates the roads from the railroad tracks. On the opposite side of the tracks is Chuck's house.

At first, I was a little nervous to enter Dawson's because it seemed so private. You couldn't see in from outside and you had to walk up some stairs to reach the corner door entrance. You can tell which residences in town used to be taverns by the front door. If you spent any amount of time walking the streets and were observant, you'd realize that there were many more bars open in the past. Dawson's had been around since the days when there were bars and taverns on almost every street corner.

19

Manayunk, was built on a hill. You can literally see seventy percent of it while driving by on the Schuylkill. It's a dirtier, more blue-collar section of the city, mostly populated by college students and the freaks that grew up there and weren't able to avoid its crappy schools. Young people like to live there because of the nightlife. Some get married and maintain a residence until they have children and either have to move to a better area or pay for private school.

I like the area because it's close to the Wissahickon. The Wiss is a roughly seven mile long gorge with a main trail that runs parallel to a stream running down its center, and a few, more narrow, trails running along both sides. The stream enters the Schuylkill River at the beginning of Fairmount Park. Fairmount leads to The Philadelphia Art Museum. If you started at the Art Museum, you could travel on trail path for over ten miles.

I prefer the Wissahickon side trails. They're more interesting and less populated. Chuck and I take his dog, Bunk, for walks there. Bunk can be off his leash for miles at a time on those trails. The side trails are where all the park's hidden treasures exist. On the north side there are these huge, long concrete water pipes that you can walk on. We use them as bridges to cross midsized gullies. There are hidden rock walls that have outlived their purpose; statues located on the top of rock formations; and a steel finger bridge that had to be lowered into place by a helicopter.

After Chuck left the phone company, he got into web development. He works from home and is able to spend time on the internet reading articles and posts by Elizabeth Warren, Robert Reich, Michael Moore, and other material that makes him crazy and helps him annoy his conservative "friends" on Facebook.

I try to expose myself to as little of this stuff as possible. I don't want to care and I feel that there's little I could do to make a difference anyway, and I could do a lot more than Chuck.

Chuck came from a large, political family that debated nightly at the dinner table. They all share the same beliefs so I'm not sure what they argued about. My guess would be to sharpen their skills. They were like a highly trained Seal team. They needed to be because they were eight of only a few dozen Democrats in their district. Everyone else was Republican. It wouldn't have been an issue if Chuck's mom wasn't a political activist and didn't make her kids work the polls every election day.

Chuck is a skinny, bald thirty something white guy. I'm glad that he's okay with his hairless head; he's lucky that it's round and proportional. I'm lucky to have a full head of hair, not just because it's better to have hair, but because I have three sets of stitches on my head and would look like a sideshow freak if I was bald.

Chuck is skilled and makes enough money to pay his bills and isn't reliant on any one individual or entity. He feels sorry for the unemployed struggling to find a job. So do I. Today's job market isn't for the faint of heart. It's hard to believe that there is less than six percent unemployment when so many jobs are being eliminated by technology and overseas outsourcing. Think about that and then attend one college graduation. Then consider that there are over two thousand colleges in the United States and graduations can occur biannually. Maybe, to help keep the unemployed from freaking out, retirement ceremonies should be made public?

It's a different world than it was for our older siblings and parents. They'll tell us that they didn't know anyone who was unemployed that didn't want to be. Or how you could make a decent living in almost any full time job.

Chuck has two brother-in-laws in opposite ends of the income spectrum: One has been unemployed, going on ten years. The other is wealthy. The rich guy was born into money. Not that he sits on his ass, though. He earned a master's degree and went to work for some other company before entering the family business. Chuck doesn't see him much because he's always working. The other brother-in-law was in a dying industry and lives in a depressed area.

If Chuck's unemployed brother in law was a woman, no one would think twice about his employment status. Chuck had a sister that didn't work for years and, according to Chuck, it wasn't a topic of conversation. It seems like society has demonized the unemployed. Maybe because no one wants it to happen to them? It's supposed to be harder to find employment when you're unemployed. It's also harder to get laid when you're not getting laid. And it cost more money to be poor. Jeez, God is a bastard.

Chuck told me that he was supposed to spend the day with his girlfriend, Britt, but she had to work. Britt's in the hospitality industry; she manages the food services at a local hotel. Chuck is amazed how hard she works for the amount of money she earns. Britt either starts work at six in the morning or two in the afternoon. If she starts at six, she'll work until four or five. If she starts at two, she'll work until "close" and "close" can be anytime, depending on what's going on at the hotel bar.

Sometimes Britt works until close one day and then opens the next morning. On those occasions she sleeps at the hotel. When Britt was hired, she was told that she wouldn't need to complete any of the actual labor. So she wouldn't have to tend bar, wait tables, deliver room service or perform barista duties at their Starbucks. Britt's a Director. She has a couple of supervisors for each department. The supervisors make a whopping twelve dollars an hour. The day-to-day employees get paid less than that. If you're offering twelve dollars or less per hour, good luck establishing a dependable workforce.

Britt came from a neighboring hotel and one of her first moves was to hire one of the employees at her old hotel and promote him to supervisor. On one of his first weekends at the new hotel, he called out. Britt's contacts informed her that the guy was working a banquet at her old hotel. Despite the new title, money is money and he knew he would make more working the banquet than supervising at Britt's hotel. Britt wanted to fire him but then she'd have to find someone else and perform all his duties in the meantime.

Frequently, Britt has had to cover for most of her subordinates. She waits tables, delivers room service, works the buffet line, mixes drinks and fills coffee orders. She works so hard; she's exhausted at the end of her shift and can barely do more than rest when she's home. She's sleep deprived. On off days, she needs to catch up on her sleep. But off days are unpredictable. If you're supposed start at six, you need to call out around four. On more than one occasion, Chuck and Britt have been awakened by Britt's phone and received the bad news that Britt will need to get her tired ass out of bed because she has to cover for one of her employees.

Britt knows she needs a new job but she's so consumed by her current position she doesn't have the energy to conduct a proper job search. Her work is affecting her health. I've wondered why obviously hard working people appear to be completely out of shape. But work is not exercise and hard, grinding work leads to poor nutrition. Britt sometimes arrives at work in the morning and won't get a break until after lunch. Unless she forced down a breakfast before heading in, she won't have time to do more than shove some unhealthy food down her throat here and there. If you're on your feet all day, the last thing you want to do is head to the gym after work, so for many weeks Britt's gym membership goes unused.

But hotels need employees and people need hotels, so what's the solution? To me, there is a wealth of MBA recipients whose only talent seems to be reducing pay and cutting labor. Think about it: If you give a determined person an almost impossible situation, that person is going to try his or her hardest to make it work. Whether it's Britt attempting to single handedly operate all of her hotel's food and beverage outlets or a sales rep with an astronomical sales quota, "quitters never win and winners never quit."

Maybe I should give that one to Chuck?

Chuck was married. He has a son who he hardly gets to see. His ex-wife and son live in California. He doesn't miss his ex, just the family life they shared. Chuck took his divorce hard and made some poor decisions during a time when he wasn't thinking clearly. He'll list them for you if you let him. He shouldn't have left the house... he shouldn't have let her move to California…he should move to California to be closer to his son… Chuck pushes a wheelbarrow of regret wherever he goes.

Ten years ago, Chuck's family was rocked hard by a tragedy that most families wouldn't recover from. I'm amazed at all that Chuck has been through and how he keeps moving forward. You never hear anything about people dealing with a pile of adversity unless things don't end well. We really should salute the people who have dealt with a large amount of shit and been able to keep it together.

The thing that Chuck envies about me isn't the money, it's that I don't seem to have a concern in the world. So I guess it might be the money indirectly. He doesn't want anything; he just doesn't want to worry. And maybe I could write a check that could make Chuck's worries disappear, and maybe I wouldn't even notice the difference in my bank statement but Chuck would never accept a payout and Chuck wouldn't be Chuck if he did. I'd lose him and he'd lose me and this is starting to sound like a Bob Seger song.

"I was watching Boardwalk Empire and it made me think. All prohibition accomplished was to make half a dozen world class bad guys rich and powerful. It sure didn't keep people from drinking," Chuck started.

This was what Chucked talked about; everything had meaning and it was never middle of the road bullshit. Chuck always came prepared, like he'd been thinking of the topic and what he was going to say ahead of time. There was no way to "win" an argument with Chuck. He debated friends for the same reason fighters had sparring partners.

"Any American with a third grade education should have been able to come to that conclusion. So why are we fighting a war on drugs?" Chuck continued.

"Do you want me to answer?"

"What do you mean?"

"I mean, eighty percent of your questions is just your way to introduce a topic or an argument."

"You mean, rhetorical questions?" Chuck said as condescendingly as possible.

We both got a chuckle out of that.

"The trouble with Americans is that they don't seem to learn from their past and can't see three steps ahead," Chuck continued, not missing a beat.

"People try to label me. I've been called a liberal, un-American, a socialist, even a communist. But I love America. I also understand we have it one hundred times better than most other countries. Go to any border town and look across to Mexico; on one side you have buildings and infrastructure and the other looks like it's recovering from an apocalypse.

"America stuck its nose in another country's business in Vietnam and what was our take away? Not that it was a terrible waste of human life and a total misuse of our tax dollars. No. It was don't conduct a draft. If you do that too many people will protest and ruin everything."

I liked listening to Chuck work out these arguments.

"But you're giving me an example of America not learning from its past. What about not being able to look a few steps ahead?" I asked. I already knew the answers, I was just being a good friend.

"I'll give America a break with prohibition. They didn't know any better. But when people want something and that something is made illegal, that spells opportunity to the people on the wrong side of the law. If Americans could get over their moral dilemma with the legalization of narcotics, the billions spent on illicit drugs, instead of that money being siphoned out of the country and into the coffers of the drug cartels, where it does absolutely no good, it could be taxed and reinvested by real American businesses.

"But, wait, it gets worse. America's not only not experiencing the benefits of that untapped revenue, we're spending billions fighting an unwinnable war on drugs.

"The typical American thinks one way: 'Drugs are bad. They should be illegal. They can't look any further down the road."

Chuck took a deep breath. His facial expression went from heavy concentration to satisfaction, like he just consumed a hearty meal or took a huge dump. Either of those two, or he was able to express all his thoughts in an organized and understandable manner.

The beer Chuck and I were drinking was taking its intended effect and all of a sudden the music in the bar sounded better and the female bartender became more attractive. Chuck was feeling the courage that alcohol affords and attempted to charm the bartender. Chuck was the one-thousandth customer to make the attempt and she deflected Chuck's appeal like a new roof repelled rain.

Our buddy John, from the phone company, entered the bar. He's older and a bit square. No matter how many times we teased him about wearing his shirts tucked in so drastically or a phone on his belt, he won't change. I'm not sure why we care.

John just returned from a trip to California. But instead of telling us about his trip, he told us about a doctor visit he had before he left.

"You know my earwax issue, right?"

Chuck shook his head. I guess he knew about it. I didn't know what I was about to hear.

"My ear was clogged *again,* so I scheduled an appointment with my doctor. It's always the same routine. They use a Waterpik to shoot water in my ear and try to force the obstruction out.

"I have a nurse practitioner. She's working on me with a nurse. One of them was pulling on my right earlobe while the other was shooting the water. I was holding a container under my ear to catch the water. I've been through this at least a dozen times. Sometimes they use warm water. Sometimes they use cold. Sometimes they mix hydrogen peroxide with the water. Sometimes they don't.

"The last time, I went to my old doctor and the nurse there kept hitting the same spot in my inner ear. It got torn up and I ended up with an ear infection."

John's in his late fifties. He's self-employed and has to purchase his own medical insurance.

"This time, it seemed like they didn't know what they were doing because they kept shooting water in there but nothing seemed to be coming out. The nurse practitioner was a little sloppy and some of the water was missing my ear and running down my neck and onto my shirt. Then she spilled the water from the Waterpik receptacle and soaked my pants."

"Sounds like a nightmare" Chuck exclaimed.

"After a few squirts, they'd stop and check my ear. The practitioner made it seem like she was making progress but I wasn't seeing much of anything in the container. After like thirty minutes, she told me that most of the wax was out and I should notice the difference after my ear dried.

"That night, it felt worse than before. So I emailed the lady and she told me to come back in. Now, the second time she made a big deal about not charging me a copay. Can you imagine any other business getting away with that crap? I go in the second time and it's more of the same. My ear is still clogged and my shirt gets soaked.

"I emailed her again, to let her know that I still had an issue and was flying to California in a couple of days. I already had to cancel a trip to Vegas because of a tooth abscess. If I had to cancel this trip... my wife... forget about it.

"The practitioner sent me to an ENT.

"I went in there and they made me pay a fifty dollar copay because they're considered a 'specialist'. I brought along an undershirt this time because I didn't want to drive home in a wet shirt.

"Well, I went in and the lady looks in my ear and I'm getting ready for the Waterpik routine. She grabs a device attached to a tube that's connected to a machine. I hear a suction sound and in two seconds my ear was completely cleared. I tell you, I was ready to kiss this lady.

"I was in and out of there in less than twenty minutes."

"Fuck yeah!"

Chuck apparently gets excited about medical breakthroughs.

"I went on my trip and I'm telling everybody about the suction device. No one cared because they weren't born with a twisted ear canal. Whatever! I got home and there were two bills waiting for me: one from my primary and a second from the ENT. I have one of those medical plans with a deductible. I owed my doctor forty-seven and the ENT another sixty. I already paid eighty bucks in copays.

"But, get this. The insurance company had to pay more than I did. Can you imagine that? How is medical insurance even affordable?"

John sat silent for a moment to let his last point sink in.

"Can you imagine any other business operating like that? I mean, what if I got into a car accident and my car got banged up. I took it to an auto body shop and they tried to fix it but couldn't and then they sent me to a special auto body shop. That place completed the job but then I received bills from both places. What other business expects to be paid even when it can't get the job done?'

"Law offices?" Chuck asked.

"Good point," John replied.

John's earwax story cleared out all the women in the bar. Chuck seemed antsy and wanted to try another establishment. John regulated himself to a predetermined number of beers. He reached that limit and was headed home. I was bored and willing so I ventured out with Chuck.

We walked west on Cresson. Cresson Street is a two way street, but people park on both sides of the road, making it just wide enough for one car to pass at a time. If you're driving down Cresson, you have to take turns pulling over for oncoming traffic. There are three bars on this stretch of road: Dawson's, the Gremlin Bar and Castle Roxx. We had to walk past the Gremlin to reach Castle Roxx.

We called it the Gremlin Bar because it was the degenerate bar in our area. I think the same ten or twelve people kept its doors open. You see them in there shortly after it opens at two and they'll be there for the remainder of the night. Most of them are straight up losers but there's one woman who stands out. She must have been cute when she was younger. Also, she carries herself with a sort of grace that's absent in the two-block radius surrounding the bar. She seems to remember me; whenever I walk past and we make eye contact, she flashes a smile. I smile back and wonder what is more interesting, the story I created in my head or how she actually ended up in such a shithole?

Chuck and I made it to Castle Roxx and because it was still early, it was as dead as Dawson's. We should have known because Castle Roxx draws a younger crowd that, due to financial constraints, must maximize their bar dollars by minimizing their bar hours. Those people were going to arrive closer to ten, when Castle's famous five-dollar shot and a beer special began. But because you can't determine the occupancy of the bar before you're inside and eye to eye with the bartender, it seemed mandatory to sit down and have at least one drink.

Castle Roxx does have an excellent jukebox (it's not really a jukebox but I don't know what else to call it). They'll even turn up the volume if you ask. That's why Chuck liked the bar. For a few bucks he could queue a dozen songs. That would give us more than enough time to get loaded. The music machine had eliminated our desire for mobility on more than one occasion.

When it's a smaller crowd everyone knows who's making the selections. Chuck is aware of that as much as he's motivated to create an enjoyable playlist. A person's taste in music is pretty much determined by his or her first selection. Chuck likes to think that people are impressed by his choices. One time, Chuck thought he loaded a Black Keys' song (at least that's what he claimed) but mistakenly chose a Black Eyed Peas' song, and not just any Black Eyed Peas' song but a remixed, hyped up version. While he was making the remainder of his selections, I could see his face getting flush and the back of his neck turning red.

Whenever I chose the music, I would take too long deciding and a few songs would play and my beer would get warm before I could sit down and enjoy them. Chuck must have memorized the music selection and planned his picks ahead of time because he would be seated before his first song completed.

Chuck intended on giving the other bar patrons a music lesson that night. His first choice was *Simple Man*, by Lynyrd Skynyrd. This was Chuck's attempt to keep that song alive with the youth of the country. Tim, the bartender was closer to our age and seemed relieved whenever Chuck commandeered the bar's music selection. It was either that or some punk would play Maroon 5.

"They have three excellent songs; this one's their best. I like the band okay but their lyrics lack subtlety," Chuck summarized.

31

Chuck and I grew up in the nineties. We were lucky to witness the Grunge era, which we both agreed was the second most important time period in the history of rock music. We were disgusted by the current state of music or what we believed represented the pussification of the American male youth.

Chuck's second song was *Dream On*, by Aerosmith. It was a little overplayed but Chuck was operating within the parameters of the limited music selection available in the music machine (I'm going with music machine).

"Name one band that could write or perform a song like this today?" Chuck rhetoricalized.

Chuck and I started out drinking draft beer but it wasn't cold enough. Chuck had an idea.

"Hey Tim, what's the strongest beer you sell?"

Tim smiled and laughed. "Did you guys walk here tonight?"

"Yes sir!" Chuck replied.

"I just had some Victory V Twelve come in. It's twelve percent, that's three times the alcohol content of regular beer, and the bottles are 750 milliliters. They go for twelve bucks a pop."

"Oh, no," I said.

"Frankly, I want to get rid of them because they're taking up too much room in my refrigerator. But be careful, drinking one bottle is the equivalent to drinking six bottles of regular beer," Tim warned us.

"Send them our way," Chuck said with a smile.

Tim brought out these enormous corked bottles with bright red labels. They looked ridiculous.

Chuck and I filled our glasses, cheered and took a gulp. "Hell yeah!" was Chuck's reaction. The beer was the strongest I've ever had. We were really getting into the IPAs and craft beers lately and they're all strong. Used to be, we'd look for the easiest drinking beers we could find and pound them like water. The colder and smoother they were, the better. We kid ourselves that we were drinking less of the hard stuff. I guess we might have been but we still drank more than normal people. Beer was our common denominator. It was the gasoline to our fire. If any of us ordered anything else, it would be equivalent to rooting against the Eagles or the Phillies. It shouldn't have mattered so much; it shouldn't have mattered at all, but it was beer and only beer.

Tim and the other bartender, Lisa, were a couple. Tim's older, balder and Lisa's sneaky cute. They were easily the nicest bartending couple in the area. But when someone discovered that they were a couple, that person tended to act shocked, at Tim's expense. Tim didn't seem to mind. If anyone got upset, it was probably Lisa for having her taste in men questioned.

Chuck's third song was *I Got Mine*, by the Black Keys. If a band from today was going to honor old rock then Chuck was definitely going to honor that band.

"You know, you really did it," Chuck said to me. "Fucking A! I saw it in you, though, when you first started at The Phone Company. I was like, 'Who does this punk think he is?' But you were cool. Anytime I needed help, you were there."

"I felt the same. There were so many dicks working there. If it wasn't for you and Eddie…"

"Fucking Eddie!" Chuck laughed. "What is wrong with that guy?"

"Come on, you know you love him."

"Maybe a little. Tell me something, what are you going to do with it all?" Chuck asked.

"What do you mean?"

"The monnneeeeyyy," Chuck answered.

"I don't know. It sort of makes me uncomfortable. It doesn't seem real."

"Your lifestyle has hardly changed. Other than disappearing for weeks at a time and not going to work every day, it's like you're living the same life. Don't you want anything?" Chuck asked.

"I don't know. I really don't. Sometimes the money makes me crazy. If I think about buying something expensive, my old brain can't handle it. I mean, a hundred thousand dollars for a car?! That's crazy and it wouldn't be that expensive. On the other hand, it's ruined simple pleasures like buying a new pair of Nikes."

"When I play the lottery I can't help but dream," Chuck commented. "I think about what I'd do with the money. I think about buying a beach house. That it would help draw my boy back to me. Finally, I'd have something over my ex. I would shower him with gifts. I try to stop myself but right up until the time that I can't even find one matching number, my life is perfect. You have all that right now."

"Maybe we should buy the beach house and move everyone in. It could be like Entourage. Who would you want to be, Turtle or Drama? You know I'm a better looking Vince."

"In your dreams."

"You ask me, Vince looked only slightly more masculine than half the girls he dated."

"He definitely would have played a Maroon 5 song tonight."

"Why isn't this easy for me? In all my dreams, I never thought having a lot of money would be so troubling."

"Everybody thinks that having money will solve all their problems when all it does is create new ones," Chuck commented.

I guess Chuck was right but all I wanted was a simple life. All my friends knew I was loaded and had ideas on how I should be living. Those opinions were based on what they thought they'd do with the money. If you polled them all, I bet not one of them, including Chuck, would handle it like I have. Chuck would use the money to rebuild his relationship with his son and get back at his ex. Eddie would live on an estate and drive around in an exotic sports car. John would retire and move to Florida. Rick would find new friends.

"If my dad had been successful, he could have bought and sold you," Chuck proclaimed.

"Ha! Good point. Surprised you brought that up." Then silence. Okay, still a sore subject to Chuck.

Chuck's next selection was The Faces, *Stay with Me*.

"This particular song got Ronnie Wood his gig with the Stones and Kenney Jones a spot in The Who, although there was no way Jones could follow Moon," Chuck proclaimed. "I mean, listen to the fucking guitar in this song. I didn't hear it at first and then I did and understood why the Stones wanted him to replace Mick Taylor. But the Stones were best with Taylor. Wait until you hear Love in Vain. Great fucking song. Even better live."

At this point, Chuck was in his own little world. He was half singing along with music while sporadically playing different musical instruments. One second he was playing guitar, the next the drums. Sometimes he sang the lead and other times the chorus. He hardly ever played the bass. It was fine, though. I was enjoying the music and happy that Chuck felt so comfortable around me.

"You okay there, buddy?" I asked Chuck, like he was a five year old.

"I'm surprised there hasn't been a band that called itself, Weapons of Mass Destruction. What a crock of shit..."

Oh, no this could go dark for Chuck.

"Why call it that? Why come up with a catchy slogan? What are weapons of mass destruction anyway? If they're nuclear bombs, why not say that? Is that too specific? Too easy to disprove? Doesn't have a ring to it? It was obviously a sales job. So why did they want to sell a war to the American public?"

Chuck has made this point to me a number of times. It was a valid one. I sure didn't have the answer. We were taught not to fight in school. If you got in a fight at school, you'd be suspended. If you got into a fight at work, you'd probably get fired. But our country gets in fights all the time. And it's not the four pushes and three roundhouse punches kind of fighting, it's the thousands of lives lost and billions of dollars flushed down the toilet variety.

The only answer I can come up with is all the money we spend on the military. We have all these highly trained troops and high tech weaponry, of course we're going to want to use them. Not doing so would be equivalent to owning a Testarossa and keeping it locked up in your garage.

Consider what we do to our soldiers. Imagine aiming a rifle at anyone, I don't care if it's a person you hate more than death, firing and witnessing that person's life vanish. What if you had to do that repeatedly, to complete strangers who might be in the same situation you're in - a soldier trying to make a life for himself. Say you're religious and had 'shalt not kill' ingrained in your head. Why would we expect any soldier to return from the battlefield and be able to lead a normal and productive life?"

What's So Funny Bout Peace Love and Understanding was next to play. Chuck was on a roll.

"Fuckin Elvis Costello…" was all Chuck could muster. Followed by, "I miss my son."

This could go one of two ways. Chuck could fall apart or he could circle the wagons around his heart and soldier through. He thought he was doing the right thing, letting his ex take his son with her to California. She had a really good opportunity, so he figured she'd be able to take better care of him. He didn't think that his son would turn against him, though. He kept reminding himself that it was a phase.

"Everything happens for a reason." Chuck found comfort in a tired maxim. "Tim! Two more magnums please."

"You sure? That beer is a creeper," Tim replied.

"What do you mean?"

"I mean, all the alcohol hasn't hit you yet. It's like time release medicine."

"Let me intervene," I intervened. "We'll have two regular Victory's. Chuck's out of his mind right now."

"Thanks mom," was Chuck's reply.

Just when Chuck was preparing himself for the first note of *Love in Vain*, The Beatles', *Love Me Do* started to play.

"What the fuck?! Goddammit! I fucking picked the wrong song. I hate this fucking song!" Chuck exclaimed.

I could tell Chuck wanted to get on a loudspeaker and inform everyone in the bar that not only did he not choose *Love Me Do*, but that he never would have selected the song. What made the situation worse to Chuck and funnier to me (I seriously almost coughed up the alcohol equivalent of two beers after witnessing Chuck's reaction.) was that *Love Me Do* was a possible selection. It was a popular, classic rock song, like Chuck's other selections. If Captain and Tennille's, *Love Can Keep Us Together* had played instead, it would have been an obvious mistake. It was killing Chuck to think that some idiot in the bar was making a mental note that based on Chuck's expert opinion, *Love Me Do* was indeed a great song.

"And people wonder how McCartney could record *That Girl is Mine* with Michael Jackson," Chuck mentioned, his voice full of disgust.

Love Me Do played for what seemed like forever. I thought Chuck was going to get up and leave the bar. Then we were saved by *Waiting Room*, by Fugazi. Relief washed over Chuck's face and the experience with *Love Me Do* gave him a second wind.

Chuck read somewhere that Fugazi was a lot of other bands' favorite band. He's been pretentious about it ever since.

"Great fucking band that no one's heard of. I don't even know how it's on the TouchTune?"

Wait, is that what it's called? Chuck knew the entire time?

I was expecting any minute for Chuck to update me on the state of his bowel movements. Chuck treated the topic no differently than if he was briefing me on the status of his stock portfolio.

"I haven't had a solid shit for over four months." Chuck didn't disappoint. "Sometimes the only reason I go is so I can have some alone time and to read. I get my best reading done in the bathroom. It's gotten to the point where if I find an article that interests me I feel the urge to go."

I had to agree, if there were no women in the world, libraries would have stalls in every aisle.

Next up, *Sliver*, by Nirvana. Chuck always played *Sliver* because he thought it was Nirvana's best song but hardly played anywhere.

Chuck was most active during this song. He alternated between Cobain and Grohl. I think if Chuck could be anyone in the history of the world, he would be Cobain. He'd even kill himself. His second choice would be Pete Townshend. If he could only pick one moment, it would be Townshend performing See Me, Feel Me at Woodstock. His second choice would be Cobain performing Sliver anywhere.

Chuck was feeling it. He spotted this dude at the bar and got all excited.

"Declan! Doesn't this guy look like Morgan Spurlock? You know, the guy from Super Size Me?"

Here was the problem. The guy did look like Morgan Spurlock but this was the third time Chuck made that discovery. Every Time Chuck got blasted at Castle Roxx, this dude would be there and Chuck would go through the same routine.

"Tim! Tim! Get us a round of shots. Make that French toast shot for us. And give one to my friend, Morgan here, and his girlfriend."

The Morgan Spurlock look alike looked like Morgan's older, tougher brother or Morgan if he just did a dime at a penitentiary. Luckily, he didn't take offense.

Tim brought over the shots. They actually were pretty tasty. I think they're the only shots I liked drinking.

Knocking on Heaven's Door, Dylan's version was the next selection. Chuck was bringing it down. He must have known that we'd be pretty juiced by that point.

"Dylan was a fucking poet. Him and Springsteen." Chuck couldn't make himself play a Springsteen song in a Philly bar, it would be too cliché, but he did have mad respect for the guy. "I was reading the lyrics to *Thunder Road* and it was impossible to not hear the song in my head. I don't know why he chose Max Weinberg, though. The guy plays drums like he only has one arm. I wish I could play *Incident on 57th Street* for you. The first time I heard it,

I thought 'that's not Weinberg' and I was right. Springsteen's first drummer was ten times better."

"Love you bro."

"Love you too," Chuck replied. "Wish you were a woman so I could make love to you."

"See there? You went and took it too far."

"Britt wants to have a baby."

"Dude! You doing it?"

"I told myself that I wouldn't have another kid. I got a son and look how I fucked that up. I mean, I need to save for retirement. That seems like an impossible dream right now."

"You're still young."

"I had to use up a lot of my buyout money to get my business going. I'm making money now but it's not like I don't know what to do with it all. We have a child... that cost thousands."

"It's like school; when you're going through it, it doesn't seem like so much, but if you had to do it all over again, you'd probably look for a tall building to jump off of."

"Good analogy," Chuck replied. "Britt really wants to be a mom. I can't take that away from her but if I don't want another kid... To me, it seems pretty simple. If she wants a kid and I don't, we should split up, but that doesn't seem to be an option. Ever wonder why someone loves you? Why am I such a prize? Britt adores me and I'm a jerk to her half the time. My first wife hated me and I wasn't half as jerky."

We stewed on that thought for a bit.

Say it Ain't So was Chuck's last tune. He claimed that song was the most affected by alcohol consumption. A person's enjoyment of the song was directly proportional to the amount of alcohol he or she consumed.

I could hear some of the other bar patrons singing along. Chuck had won over the crowd.

What happened in the next hour was a blur but Chuck and I ended up at the Gremlin Bar and I got to sit next to the mysterious smiling woman.

So what happened? How did this seemingly normal woman end up as a regular at the creepiest bar in Manayunk?

Here's the version of the story I made up in my head:

Her husband was a computer industry pioneer. He envisioned the laptop computer when the only computers in existence were huge mainframe computers the size of small buildings. He was an executive for IBM but decided to start his own company. With his reputation and vision, he had no problem securing funding. The Gremlin Queen was living the good life in New York City. They lived in Manhattan's Upper East Side. Their two boys went to the Browning School and they were members at Saint Andrews. Then her husband had a stroke and ended up in a home; the banks called in their loans; their investors bailed; the Queen had no marketable skills or work history; the family was decimated. She had to move back to Pennsylvania, and in with her mother. She started drinking and hadn't stopped since.

This is what actually transpired:

"Hi," I said cautiously.

"Hiiii," she droned back.

"I see you here when I walk by," I offered.

"Realllly?" she replied.

Oh great, she hadn't noticed me.

"Yeah, you always give me a nice smile."

"I like to smmiile."

41

CHAPTER 3

—◄○►—

I GUESS I NEED TO TELL YOU what happened; how I became so wealthy. To do that, I need to go back to my middle school days.

I was always an athlete. There were eleven boys, all about the same age, living on my street growing up. We didn't need to join Little League or Pop Warner to play football, basketball or baseball. Our games were played in our backyards or at a local park.

I excelled in our informal competition but struggled in organized sports. At the same time, my father was a running nut. He got caught up in the running boom that started in the seventies. He ran a few marathons but he was nothing more than a plodder; he'd be lucky to break four hours. He used to show me videos of classic footage of different track meets, marathons and cross country races. He had quite the collection. He attended collector events to find the stuff. My dad had me read *Best Efforts*, by Kenny Moore; Bill Rodgers and Marty Liquori's autobiographies; *Pre*, by Tom Jordan... My dad wanted to name me "Eamonn", after Eamonn Coghlan but my mom wouldn't let him. They compromised. My mom chose Declan and my dad chose "Walker" for my middle name, after New Zealand's great miler, John Walker.

In middle school, after failing to make the basketball team and getting tossed out of wrestling, I decided to go out for track. During the very first practice, one of the coaches told me I had a nice stride. I was hooked. Nothing I did up to that point or since made my dad happier.

By the time I started running, the Africans had taken over the sport. Gone, it seemed, were all the personalities from the seventies and eighties. Maybe that was true or the kids that made up my demographic couldn't relate to the African runners. And I was the only runner I knew who cared about the old timers.

I guess I'm a dreamer. When I trained, in my brain I was Pre or Rodgers. I didn't just absent-mindedly finish a training run. There was a short tunnel that went under the train tracks, down the street from my parents' house. I ran through it at the end of most of my training runs. Every time I ran I approached the tunnel I heard network commentary in my head.

First Announcer:

"Jim, Declan has a two minute lead on the competition and he's finishing strong. All he has to do is make his way into the Olympic stadium and one and a half laps around the track and the gold medal is his. Barring tragedy, this race is over."

Jim:

"No one really challenged Declan today. This is the result of years and years of hard work and struggle. This kid earned everything he's ever achieved. Look at him, he's twenty-five miles in and he's still running as smooth sheet metal."

I wore white work gloves, like Rodgers, in the winter and a

painter's hat, like Dick Beardsley. I tried to grow my hair long, like Prefontaine. I would have been so happy if my high school or college uniforms were all black, like New Zealand's.

I was a good runner but not great. I was a little big for a distance runner and not fast enough to excel in the middle distances. But I was a competitor and won a fair share of my races in high school. The problem was, for a runner at my talent level, I took it way too seriously. To me, running and competing were more important than school or anything else. If I applied myself, I probably could have gotten into any college I wanted to. I scored near perfect in my math SATs and I purposely missed some questions.

I chose a small liberal arts college because the cross country coach there recruited me. Big mistake. I would have been far better off attending a university where the majority of my classes would be in mathematics and engineering. I skated through high school without trying. That didn't happen in college. I skipped most of my classes but never missed a training run. I barely made it through my freshman year and screwed my GPA. It didn't help matters that I spent my summers lifeguarding instead of interning. Also, I sort of wigged out during my junior year and decided it would be a good idea to 'get away' and spend a semester at the University of Arizona, in Tucson. I ended up in a hall full of crazies, partying my ass off.

I was almost unemployable when I graduated college. Luckily for me, the local phone company was hiring and based most of their selection criteria on an assessment test administered to all the applicants. I scored very high and was hired to be a sales engineer. It was my job to go on appointments with the dopey sales reps and duel it out with IT managers.

Eddie and I started at the phone company right after the dotcom bubble burst. Chuck and Rick started a few years prior, when the phone company was more of a monopoly. Eddie's always been a cocky bastard. Somehow he talked his way into an outside sales position. One of AT&T's best customers, a large movie theater chain, put out an RFP for their network. Everyone thought AT&T was entrenched. Nobody in our sales department thought we had a chance to win the business so Eddie and I, the new guys, were given the opportunity.

I don't think the movie theater company thought we had a chance either because all their money guys skipped our meeting. It was just me and Eddie and the IT guys from the theater company. I guess I had one of those moments because after listening to the tech guys describe their existing network, I went up to a whiteboard and diagrammed a network that required twenty percent less circuits but was more robust, scalable, secure and redundant. Eddie was mostly quiet the entire meeting; after the introductions he made just one comment. After listening to the theater guys tell us what a nightmare AT&T's implementation was years prior, how it took close to a year and how the executives at the company thought it should have been completed in weeks (totally unrealistic), and after I described a similar project we had worked on, Eddie deadpanned, "Took us two weeks." That busted up the tech guys and the deal was all but ours.

The tech guys told us that they had to go through the entire RFP process, but that we should base our submittal on the network I designed not the one requested in the RFP. They knew all the other bidders would come in higher than our company. If our price was lower and we got their seal of approval we'd win the deal.

Eddie and I kept it cool for the remainder of our meeting and walk down the hallway towards the elevator but I'm pretty sure the

IT people could hear us celebrating on the other side of the elevator door. We couldn't believe it. With little help from our department, we were going to win a multimillion dollar deal.

When we arrived back to our office, Sherry asked, "How did it go?"

Eddie's sales manager, Sherry, should have attended our meeting but he told us we could handle it. If it amounted to anything, she'd get involved.

"Boss, it was just me and Declan and the IT guys. Declan went up to the whiteboard and you would have thought he sculpted fucking David right in front of them."

"What did I tell you about your use of profanity?" Sherry replied.

"Oh, sorry. I'm just excited." Eddie apologized.

"You think there might be something to it?"

"He...ck yes! They told us to bid out Declan's design. Everyone else will be pricing out something similar to what AT&T has in place now. Also, turns out they're not nuts about Ma Bell."

"Very nice," Sherry responded.

At that point, a few others, including Rick, had congregated just outside of Sherry's cubicle.

"Hey Rick, you should have worked that theater lead! Declan and Eddie think we have a good shot," Sherry proclaimed.

"Bullshit!" Rick responded.

"What is it with all of you and your language?" Sherry interrupted.

"Sorry boss. We're not used a female sales manager, that's all," Rick explained.

"I don't think so, Rick," Eddie proclaimed. "Declan put on a show for the folks over there. He had them eating out of his hand."

"Fuck me... Oh, shit, sorry boss," Rick replied. "You know, good for you guys, but I wouldn't start counting your chickens."

Eddie and I ended up closing the theater deal, which lead to deals with other theater chains. Eddie made President's club for like six straight years. Eventually, he went out on his own and leveraged those relationships to build a successful telecom consulting agency.

Rick scratched and clawed his way into a sales engineer position but had to go back into sales when the company merged with another phone company. John was a lifer. Those were the people that worked their entire careers at the phone company. He started working for the phone company, right out of high school. Back then, the union was still strong. Later on, John accepted a buyout and started his own phone equipment company. He and Eddie worked on a number of deals together.

Chuck was like me; he started with the phone company after college. He accepted a buyout the same time Rick went back into sales. Chuck got into web development and started his own company.

I became a bit of a legend at the phone company. About the same time Chuck accepted his buyout and Rick was being pushed back into sales, my title was Senior Lead Engineer in the Global Accounts department. The only customers I worked with billed more than a million dollars a year with the company.

Around that same time, two guys I knew from the University of Arizona were developing a movie app. The app was sort of like Pandora for movies. If a user entered their five favorite movies, directors and actors, it could predict, with a very high degree of certainty, whether or not a person would enjoy a particular movie. It was a cute little app that probably would have been lost in a big *scrapp* heap somewhere if those guys hadn't read an article about my work with the movie theaters.

They were in town and we met for dinner one night and I had another whiteboard moment.

"If your app can tell people what movies they'd like, wouldn't it be a good tool for people to use to meet each other?" I asked.

James, known as "James from New York" and Kyle, whose real middle name was "Pardy" lived on my floor at the U of A.

It was the spring semester of my junior year. The bus company lost my bags during my bus ride (I was trying to save my parents money) from Philly to Tucson. I had just spent three and half straight days on a moving Greyhound. At about three days in, the rate of motion became so ingrained in my brain that I was pretty sure I could walk alongside the moving bus. Also, my hair was so thick and greasy, I looked like a claymation character.

I had reserved a single room, but at some point during the two-mile walk from the bus station to campus, I thought that since I didn't know anyone, I should have a roommate. That decision lead me to a hall full of knuckleheads and what would have been a lifelong struggle with drug addiction, if I had such a propensity.

My roommate was a rich kid from Washington, DC. The first thing he did every morning was light up a pipe next to his bed. He was waking and baking before the term was invented. I don't think I ever saw him with clear eyes. James was in the next room. He used to cut his t-shirts into t-shirt vests and somehow pulled off the look. Kyle lived off campus but might as well have lived on our floor, he was there so much. One kid on our hall was an American Indian and if he ever drank, we'd all be in for it. To him, James from New York, was from another planet. New York was a mythical place he could only dream of. The Indian got drunk one evening and spent the rest of the night out on the fire escape, screaming, "James! James from New York! ...James from New York City!" over and over again.

There was another guy from Georgia that swung by our hall on occasion. He didn't drink or do traditional drugs. He was a huge fan of Robitussin. He called it Robo. He would slam six ounces of the stuff. He told us it had close to the same chemical makeup of morphine. We thought he was nuts. One night, James and I were bored and didn't have any pot and nobody was going out so we tried it. Nothing. We didn't feel a thing. Like idiots we decided to try it again the next day. For the next two days we were stoned. James and I laid in our beds like invalids. The only thing we could manage to do was walk to the restroom. James had the brilliant idea of smoking some pot on the second day. For about an hour I was sure I fried my brain. There were two older kids on my street that did that. I remember watching them walk up and down our street like zombies. I thought for sure I'd be the next. Thankfully, we came down on the third day.

There was another kid from Texas in our hall. He ran a four-ten mile in high school. In other words, he could have kicked my ass. He looked like a cross between Mick Jagger and Keith Richards. Girls used to fight for his attention. There were a few others but any thoughts of studying flew out my dorm window during my first week on campus. It was a mile walk to the library and only a half mile to one of our favorite bars. Every night we went out and every night we sucked down two pitchers each. I had worked in the one of the school's kitchens but I quit when the job cut into my party time. After my meal card ran out, I existed on a diet of Jack in the Box burgers and beer. I sold my plasma and some of my clothes for spending money.

I ended up with three C's, a D and an incomplete. I entered one final an hour late, wearing mirrored sunglasses. Another, I hadn't even opened the textbook. I was a goner but there weren't enough desks and a girl, by the grace of God, laid on the floor right beneath me to complete the exam. I copied her answers verbatim.

We met a drug dealer about three quarters through the semester. One night, it was line after free line of coke. I had him sleep over in my roommate's bunk because I wanted to hang with him the following day. After a night of coming down and no sleep, to get rid of him, I told him I forgot I had to work that day. I never talked to the guy again. My roommate and Kyle were hooked, though. One night they came back to the hall and told us all that the dealer asked if he could give them both head. They swore they'd never return. Two days later they went back. I remember my roommate returning to our room at five one morning, wasted, the same day he had a math final.

At the end of the semester I waited for my mom and sister to pick me up and drive me home. I had to scurry back to the liberal arts college to have any hope of graduating. I guess Kyle cleaned himself up and he and James got working on their app.

CHAPTER 4

W HEN I GOT INVOLVED, THE MOVIE app was pretty basic. It was nice to be able to enter any movie title in the app and have it spit out the percent chance that you would enjoy it. The app had a fair amount of downloads and website traffic.

What got me thinking was my personal dating history and how important similar movie taste was to the success of a relationship. Every girl that I dated for any significant amount of time enjoyed the same movies that I did. On the other hand, I once dated a woman that wouldn't let me talk during *Starsky and Hutch* because she didn't want to miss anything. I broke up with another girl after she informed me that she walked out of *Something About Mary*.

Just liking movies period was important. If a woman didn't like to stay home and watch a movie, she probably wasn't a good match, at least for me.

But what about a movie as a first date? Most people believe that a first date at the movies isn't a good idea. They maintain that a couple should make eye contact and converse during a first date and a movie isn't conducive to either. But that was another issue we could resolve.

Before they even met, the couple would know they shared similar tastes; they'd have something to discuss after watching the movie; and a movie could help eliminate much of the first date pressure.

I leveraged my relationships with the movie theater industry to integrate their ticket and concession purchasing data. Our app would inform the user what theater would be ideal based on a number of criteria: the location in relationship to both parties, number of tickets sold, movie times, traffic and price. A user would be offered their two best options and they could purchase their tickets and snacks before they left home. They were provided turn by turn directions to the theater. When they arrived at the theater, there were no lines. They walked right into the theater and their concessions were waiting for them. Roses and exotic chocolates were added to the list of concessions, helping the theaters increase their revenues.

It turned out that a couple's first date experience could add to the level of attraction that they felt for one another. If everything went smoothly and the movie was a hit, both parties associated those feelings with the other individual. The success of our dating site wasn't just measured by the number of users and amount of revenue it generated, but also by the number of resulting marriages. MovieDate ended up crushing the competition.

MovieDate eliminated most of the skeeviness of internet dating. Since the minimum commitment was the time required to watch a movie, our service discouraged the people who were just looking to hook up. Initial conversations were about movie tastes, so men were less likely to request nude photos or send dick pics.

What really helped was that our site was written into the script of a summer blockbuster. And not just a big budget movie with gobs of marketing dollars behind it, but an entertaining and memorable feature; the type that people recite lines from and watch over and over again. Two of the characters met using our service. Anyone on a date, watching the movie would have the trippy experience of watching two people meeting using a movie themed, dating website. People left the theater, went home and looked us up on the web. When they found out we were a real website, our usership took off.

After the movie exposure and my contribution our user base went from thousands to millions and revenue skyrocketed. Our service had been credited with single handedly saving the movie theater industry. Many folks that were previously watching movies at home were now going on movie dates.

It was also the perfect time to be involved with a successful web service. Google and Facebook were driving up the values of businesses like ours. There was much to do about our purchase price but it was made with mostly overvalued stock shares. The minute I was allowed to cash in my shares, I did so.

CHAPTER 5

◄○►

CHUCK AND I WERE MEETING OUR friends, Rick and Eddie, for lunch at one of the best cheesesteak joints in Philly, Dalessandro's.

Dalessandro's is so popular the owners can't afford to shut the place down long enough to remodel and transform it into a real restaurant. From open to close, there's a nonstop line of people ordering steak sandwiches. But there's no place to sit without experiencing a waiting customer's crotch two feet from your face.

The place is no bigger than the inside of a good sized cargo container but inside there's a full kitchen, a dining counter, about six employees, four refrigerators and a few skinny tables. When you're inside, you can't find a place to stand or sit without being in someone's way.

You have fight your way through a mass of mostly overweight freaks to order your food (they won't let you pay when you order for some reason) find somewhere to stand, wait until your name's called and then fight your way back through a different set of chubs to pick up your food and pay. If you leave a tip, the person helping you will say, "Let's thank Declan." and then the rest of the employees will shout, "Thank you Declan!"

Dallesandro's has no parking lot, undersized dining tables, a small counter area, won't accept credit cards, and probably brings in more revenue than any other dining establishment in a ten mile radius.

I've never been in the place when there wasn't a line and a chaotic group of people hovering around the line. On the grill, there was always a two-foot high pile of shredded meat, a foot high pile of onions and a stack of cheese that looked like more cheese than could be eaten in one day by a hundred people.

Why would we pick this place, especially when there are at least ten other restaurants that served cheesesteaks in the general area? Because the cheesesteaks at Dalessandro's seem to melt in your mouth. I've had steaks at dozens of other places but after tasting the ones at Dalessandro's, I won't go anywhere else.

We engaged in small talk as we were pushed around by the steak crowd. It felt like standing in the ocean during high tide. After we got our food we grabbed an empty picnic table outside the restaurant.

"Fucking A, right?" Rick exclaimed as we sat down. "I can't believe that place. How many steaks do you think they sell a day?"

Eddie, Chuck and I contemplated Rick's question but none of us bothered to answer.

Rick is shorter, dark and sort of handsome. He was always well dressed and looked out of place at a shop like Dalessandro's. He was a decent account manager; he got out of direct sales for a bit but had to go back. He was a bit more fun back in the day but now seemed a little uneasy about his future.

"They're the best," Eddie followed. "I don't trust Pat's because it doesn't look like they ever clean the place. Geno's? It's so garish and

I'm not sure what's going on over there with the 'You have to order in English' crap."

Eddie was the most dynamic of the four of us. He was tall, slumpy, blond and blue eyed. Eddie was always tan and looked like he belonged at the beach. Most people thought Eddie was from California.

Everyone was always asking Eddie where he was from because of the way he spoke. Some guessed Boston, some Australia. But he was from right here, in Philly. He sort of made up his own accent.

"I like the Rocky remembrance at Pat's," Chuck proclaimed. Pat's had a plaque where you stood to order that read, "On this spot stood Sylvester Stallone filming the great motion picture Rocky, Nov, 21, 1975."

"Have you ever had one from Pat's and then walked across the street and had another one from Geno's?" Rick asked.

"I'm surprised anyone can look down and see their privates in this town with all the shit food we eat. You have the steaks, Tastykake, Wawa, pizza, soft pretzels… all garbage." Eddie proclaimed.

"Britt's on a low carb diet," Chuck shared.

"She should be on a low food diet," Eddie fired.

"Right this second, I wish you would start a low oxygen diet," Chuck fired back.

And Eddie wondered why Chuck had issues with him.

"You know, I invented low carb," Eddie proclaimed.

"Here we go," Rick warned us.

"I'm telling you the truth. I've been pointing out to people for years how cows eat nothing but grain and are fat and lions eat nothing but meat and are lean and muscular. Which would you rather be a cow or a lion?"

"Okay Eddie Atkins," Chuck quipped.

"Yesterday, I must have scratched my ass for two solid minutes," Eddie followed.

You had to wonder how we could continue eating after hearing some of our topics of discussion.

"I mean, I wipe and wipe... I get right in there with soap when I take a shower. I don't know if it's that my asshole is so itchy or I just enjoy it?" Eddie continued.

"You never really see women scratching the inside of their assholes," Rick pointed out.

"Or hear them fart," Chuck offered. "Bunk and I do all the farting in my house."

"How's sales?" Eddie asked Rick.

"Fuck man... Nothing's easy anymore. You know, when we all worked together, you had to work but it was doable. Go to work, bust ass, kick ass and leave it all behind until you came back the next day. Now, you don't get that same feeling of accomplishment, even if you make a sale, because as soon as one comes in, you start worrying about the next one."

Eddie, Chuck and I were happy to be away from all that.

"I do better than most but I'm barely making it. I've got just enough money to live. I'm freakin' afraid to buy anything particularly expensive. My girlfriend's on me about never going anywhere and I'm like 'what's wrong with staying home?' I don't know how some schlub working at Acme's doing it."

Rick stopped himself because he didn't want to make it sound like his life was worse than ours. Money and success had become sort of a sore subject amongst the four of us.

"You should go out on your own," Eddie offered.

Eddie left the phone company a few years ago and started his own telecom agency. It was easy for him to say, though because he was able to take some large accounts with him when he left.

Eddie probably regretted that suggestion as soon as the words came out of his mouth. There was a lot of things that Rick should have done.

"Easy for you to say," Rick fired back.

It was getting harder and harder for the four of us to hang out together. Back in the day, these lunches were a daily ritual. But then the subject matter would have been some girl's tits, stories about hooking up, Swingers, or some other movie we loved; no one would be bitching about money or the economy. Well, maybe Chuck.

"It's gotta be tough to make it in sales these days. America is losing its customer base" Chuck chimed in.

"Oh, no." I said, sensing Chuck was ready to cut loose with one of his diatribes.

"No, really. What's better, one guy making ten million a year or two hundred making fifty grand?" Chuck didn't wait for an answer. "If you have two hundred people all making fifty grand, they all need cars, housing, clothes, food… One guy making millions can only buy so much. That person is not going to spend the same percentage of his income. Fucking trickle-down theory. Why do people buy that crap?"

Eddie, Rick and I ate a quarter of our sandwiches while Chuck's mouth was busy talking. Luckily it was clear before he started or we would have probably been showered by tiny steak particles.

"What's that got to do with selling phone service?" Eddie asked Chuck.

"It's got a lot to do with it. The Phone Company generates the majority of its revenue selling to other businesses," Chuck responded. "If the business world is struggling the phone company will struggle also."

"It's not about working hard. It's about being smart. If you can't make ends meet working at Acme, get a better job," Eddie suggested.

"Not everyone can afford college, Eddie. And some people just aren't cut out to own their own telecom agency or build websites. I mean, the world still needs grocery clerks," Chuck replied.

"I have to figure something out," Rick continued. "I don't know how my parents did it. I mean my mom and dad put four kids through college, paid off their mortgage and had enough to retire. Maybe I'm spending too much on cable?"

"Yeah, it's probably cable TV's fault," Chuck baited.

"No really. My parents didn't get divorced. They didn't spend money on cafe lattes, premium channels and smartphone apps. I bought them their first color TV. Shit, when I was living at home we didn't own a clothes dryer. Maybe it's our fault? Maybe we're wasting our money on crap?"

"Used to be, any self-respecting salesman wouldn't think twice about making a purchase," Eddie proclaimed. "My first sales director encouraged us to get into debt."

"Look, we're a buy it on credit society" Chuck explained. "My parents were the same as Rick's; they didn't buy something unless they had the money in the bank. But, we sort of have to be this way. Used to be, one income was all it took. Then the spouse had to go to work as well. Everyone is working harder and earning less, and everything costs more."

"You know when we were young, we never talked about this shit," Eddie said. "Now, every time I'm around you guys, it's the same crap, 'I can't make sales', 'The economy sucks.' Man up. We're doing okay.

Chuck you have your own business. Look at fucking Declan over there. Rick, you just need to get out of telecom. It's turning into a commodity; it's all about price now."

I wanted to change the subject but had to choose my words carefully. I didn't have Rick and Chuck's problems. It would be easier for me to only hang with people that didn't have money troubles but these were my guys.

"Check out that ass" I said and drew their attention to one of the only nice bottoms visiting Dalessandro's.

"Nice!" Eddie replied.

Just like that, I got their minds off the economy.

CHAPTER 6

―◁○▷―

E DDIE'S TAKING ME TO HIS GYM today. Normally, if I lift, I do it at home. I have a bench and some weights but I'm not nuts about it. I mostly hike, bike and run. I was always a little stocky. It was tough for me to keep my weight down when I was racing. I don't need weights like Eddie does.

Eddie was a string bean growing up. In high school, some upperclassman said he looked like Gumby when he ran. The name stuck until Eddie was an upperclassman and one of the best runners in his area.

Eddie started lifting weights when he was twelve, when his dad bought him a cement set from Sears. Then his dad would question the exercise. "He bought me the weights and then he would see me lifting and say stuff like, 'If you need exercise, I have some wood you could chop.'"

Eddie lifted because he was desperate to put some meat on his bones. He had enough to deal with, with his bad skin, teeth and hair. At least he could work on his body.

Eddie's not obsessive about it, though. He's never taken any PEDs and he doesn't spend hours in the gym. He's just consistent. Eddie estimates that he's missed less than six weeks of weight training in his entire adult life. And it shows. Eddie is lean and muscular; it doesn't look like he has an ounce of fat on his body. Of course he'll tell you that, "I don't have an ounce of fat on my body." He's also willing to arm wrestle just about anyone.

"You need to develop some muscle mass," Eddie insisted. "It will speed up your metabolism. Muscle mass burns calories even when you're sleeping," he claimed.

Eddie kept telling Chuck that Britt should lift weights. The subject of Britt's weight was off the table with Chuck, though. Eddie would start up and Chuck would give him a look to let him know that he better stop.

We headed to the nearby LA Fitness, in Andorra. There was one closer, on City Line but Eddie said that was more like a prison gym. "Less riff raff at Andorra. They had to take the basketball court out of the other one because of all the fighting."

To get to Andorra, you head down Kelly Drive. Kelly is a pretty road, with rolling hills that runs alongside the Wissahickon. Traveling on the road with any sense of purpose can be frustrating. "This light is red for no reason," Eddie pointed out. Dopey drivers clogged the road like plaque obstructed an obese man's arteries. "Slow people only hustle when they're trying to get in your way," Eddie proclaimed. Driving down Kelly did give me an idea of how long my hikes can be. It's a good drive to the road that leads you to Valley Green and I've walked there a number of times.

LA Fitness is one of those corporate gyms. Eddie swears by them. He travels some for business and can go to any of their locations, across the country. He'll start listing the ones he's been to if you let him. I'm required to give them my name and other information and sit down with one of their representatives in order to receive my "free" guest pass.

You're a smart guy. I don't need to tell you how to lift," Eddie offered.

"I know the basics. I just thought, since you've been lifting for so many years that you could show me your routine and it would be fun to go to the gym together," I responded.

"Okay. Why don't I treat you like you don't know anything then?"

"Sounds good."

Eddie spelled out his workout philosophy for me: "I work chest, back, some shoulders, legs and abs. Then I take a day off and work arms, some more shoulders, legs and abs. Some guys like to work chest, shoulders, triceps, quads and abs one day and then come back the next day and work back, biceps, hamstrings and abs again. I don't like that routine because you end up walking around unbalanced. And if you have to miss a day, you're screwed. Plus, everyone works chest on Mondays and Thursdays. You're lucky if one bench is available."

"We'll do my chest and back workout today," Eddie started. "I do two exercises for my chest and back and one for my shoulders, legs and abs. I only do one exercise for my shoulders, legs and abs because I work those muscles every time I go to the gym.

"The most important key to success with resistance training is consistency. You have to make it a routine. Exercise should be as much a part of your life as eating and sleeping. You'll never get anywhere if you miss weeks at a time on a regular basis. So how do you accomplish that? First thing, don't use a trainer. Trainers like to prove themselves. You ever hear people say, 'My trainer kicked my ass this morning'? Well, how likely is it that you'll keep at something that kicks your ass?

"All you have to do is break your body into six parts: your chest, back, shoulders, arms, legs and abs. The first time you go to a particular gym, know where the machines are that will exercise each of those muscle groups. Then do two exercises per muscle group, two or three times each week.

"Whatever you do, mix it up. You have to shock your body," Eddie emphasized the word "shock" and sounded like Captain Kirk calling for Spock. "Some of these dopes insist on working the same machines every time they come in. You can tell which ones because they'll sit and wait for the machine you're working on. It's worse when they ask to work in. Never let anyone work in. They're probably going to take too long between sets and waste your time."

This was Eddie's home. He walked around the gym without an ounce of self-consciousness. He kept to himself, though. "A bunch of these guys come in to shoot the shit and hangout. I'll get more done in an hour then they will in two. I'll be on my third exercise and they're still working on their first."

There are certain gym behaviors that drive Eddie crazy. Like if someone ties up two pieces of equipment at the same time. It makes him nuts when he's about to start an exercise and "some clown" comes up and tells him he's working on the machine. "They say they're doing 'supersets', such bullshit. Just do one exercise at a time. You don't need to do supersets. That's trainer bullshit. A guy will come up and tell me he's already using a piece of equipment I was about to use. I get so annoyed, Most people would apologize and find a different piece of equipment. Not me. I have to whip out something like, *why don't you tell me what equipment you're not using?*"

Mobile phone use also drives Eddie crazy. "You want to get on a machine and some dope is sitting there on his phone...is he going to use the machine or just using it for a place to rest?"

Eddie and I started out with abs. Eddie believes that you should lift heavy weights when you're exercising your abs, to build muscle. "Why does everyone do sets of eight to twelve when they're completing every other exercise and then do sets of fifty for abs? It doesn't make sense. I lift abs heavy and it works. Here, look at these," Eddie said as he lifted up his shirt a bit. He was right, he had nice abs.

Surprisingly, Eddie doesn't go to the gym to meet women. "They all wear headphones now. I wouldn't be surprised if they weren't even listening to music. What are you going to do, tap on their shoulder to get their attention? They won't make eye contact either. I learned that through personal experience. When I was in Phoenix, I went to a LA Fitness that must have been in a gay part of town. I think some people call it *Gay Fitness*. I have nothing against the gays, God bless 'em. It's just that I'm there for one reason, to work out. I mean, I do like to look at the ladies but I'm not going to bother them. Anyway, after visiting that gym, I got an idea what women go through. I didn't want to make eye contact and what might seem like a simple request could turn into some come on. 'Hey, can I work in?' and the next thing you know some guy is trying to make conversation with you. There were so many gays in that gym, the first thing I needed to do when I walked out was look at some women. Thankfully there was a Trader Joe's in the same shopping center. I went in there afterwards and checked out the hot homemakers to clear my brain. It's like when you hear a shitty song and want to hear a good one right after so you won't go around singing the shitty one."

That's not to say that Eddie hasn't met women in the gym. "See that woman over there. the muscular one? I fucked her."

"You like that?"

"Not particularly, but I'll try anything, and it sort of fell in my lap."

"What do you mean?"

"We got to talking one day and she asked me about the lifting gloves I was wearing. I used to wear gloves when I lifted but not anymore. It was a pain in the ass, taking them on and off and you really only needed them back when the bars were more abrasive. I guess they changed them, I don't know. I think I told her I got them at Dick's, or someplace and she asked me to text her the name of the brand. I was pretty sure it was a way for her to get me to start texting with her. Then she said, 'don't text me after five.' Well that made it pretty obvious. So we start texting and the next thing I know she's coming over for a visit."

"What was it like?"

"Different. It was nice that she didn't have an ounce of fat on on her body but if she didn't have long hair there were times when I would have thought I was fucking a guy."

"You ever going to settle down?"

"I don't know."

"Don't you want to be in a relationship?"

"I've been in relationships. I'm always looking for one of those."

"Really?"

"Sure. I love getting into a relationship but my goal is to end them and have another ex."

"What?!"

"Ex-girlfriends are the best. You just have to make sure you don't end the relationship badly and then keep in touch and become friends."

"Why's that?"

"Look, women like sex just as much as men do. Keep telling yourself that. But they don't want to look or act like whores. So they can't be hooking up every time they go out or with guys from work and all that. Who better to go to when you're a horny woman? An ex. You already know each other and you've probably done it a bunch of times. They can rationalize that it was just some sort of personality conflict; if it wasn't for that you'd still be together.

"Always stay in touch with your ex-girlfriends. Always be sweet and supportive. Like their Facebook posts and that sort of crap. Next thing you know, one of them will send you a late night text and you're in business."

"You are something else. Have you considered taking this show on the road?"

"Hey, I keep these secrets to myself. You're the only one I share them with. And just like your money, they just sit unused."

"For all you know," I responded, but he was right.

After we were finished with abs we did legs. "You have to do legs!" Eddie explained. "So many dopes come in here and only work their upper bodies. They make themselves believe that walking and standing all day is enough. They look ridiculous. You can tell the ones that do that; they wear sweatpants in the summer or long ass baggy shorts.

"You don't have to go crazy with the legs; I just do one exercise, maybe four sets, but I do one every time I go to the gym. Oh, and one for your calves too. Some of these guys look like they're walking around on pegs, their calves are so puny."

Eddie loaded some weights on a leg press machine. It was sort of a pain because he had to take a couple off every time it was my turn, but Eddie was okay with it. He was happy to have me there with him. It seemed like college was the last time we exercised together.

Looking at Eddie now, it's hard to believe he was a long distance runner in college. He's over six feet and had to weigh close to two-hundred pounds. He still runs, now and then. "I don't really like it because it makes me lose weight. That and I can still run fast; the trouble is my lungs can't keep up with my legs. I get going and the next thing I know, it feels like my lungs are going to explode. My only regret is I didn't run a marathon when I was in college. They told us we couldn't run one because it would have taken too long to recover, and then we wouldn't be able to run all the silly races our coaches wanted us to. By the end of our senior year, my achilles were shit. It took me two years to run without a limp," Eddie summarized.

I looked up to Eddie in college. I could hang with him during training runs but in any distance over the mile, he had me beat. Eddie ran the five thousand meters races in our school's tri meets, against other small colleges like Moravian and Baptist Bible Bullshit. It was usually him and maybe three or four other guys. The meet would be over at that point. No one really wanted to stick around and watch some dudes battle it out for fifteen minutes or so. Eddie sometimes let the other runners hang with him for a lap or two and then it would feel too slow and he would take off. A couple of times, Eddie lapped everyone else in the race. He shouldn't have gone division three. But we were recruited by the same coach and our school was supposed to be one of the top small private colleges in the country.

Eddie and I both took college running too seriously. I barely got my math degree and, as Eddie liked to say, he majored in sales.

"Eddie how come you never got remarried?"

"You kidding me? After what happened the first time?"

"Come on, you were young and that was just a crazy turn of events. Wasn't there anyone that made you consider a second try?"

"Maybe Sofia."

Sofia was an Hispanic woman Eddie met at the gym. (So much for his headphone theory.) They dated for two years. She was born in Mexico and her father was a mine worker. She grew up in Ajo, Arizona, which was a tiny little town, south of a slightly bigger town, Gila Bend. Ajo is so small it can't support a McDonald's or Burger King. It can, however, support the billboards advertising those two Gila Bend establishments, thirty miles north.

Sofia attended graduate school in Philadelphia and was working for a local university when Eddie met her. Their relationship became serious quickly, which was the way everything happened with Eddie. Right after they met, they were spending every sleeping moment together.

"Oh yeah, what happened with her? You two were close. I really liked her."

"She was a sweetheart, no doubt about it. It was night and day compared to the first wife. But you know me... Something changed inside of me after what happened. I've never been the same."

Eddie would never utter his first wife's name. He talked about everything but her.

"All I wanted, since I was twelve, was to have a girlfriend. Then I finally got one and it was the type that screws you up permanently. Sofia was a great girl. I think if I had met her first, we'd still be together. She would have been the perfect mom. But I'm so fucked up that as soon as I'm in some sort of committed situation, I feel trapped and want to get out. I'd be with her, we'd break up, I would want her back, we'd get back together and I would want to break up again. Man, what I put that poor girl through."

"Don't beat yourself up too much."

"One of her sisters was lesbian. She had two brothers, but it was the lesbian sister that made it clear to me that I'd better stop treating her sister that way. I thought she was going to kick my ass and she was half my size.

"Her family was so close. I guess it was their upbringing. There was seven of them living in this tiny house. I went there for Christmas one time and most of the family slept on the living room floor. One time her dad came for the weekend. We were all sitting on the couch together and then he said he was ready for bed. He got up and laid down on the carpet, on the other side of our dining room table and fell asleep. I couldn't believe it. He couldn't speak a lick of English but what a great guy. He put four kids through college and two of them got their graduate degrees. Anyone that says anything bad about Hispanics doesn't know what they're talking about."

"You ever talk to her?"

"Now and then, a text here or there but I have to let her alone. I wish she'd find the perfect guy. She deserves it...

"Hey, we're supposed to be working out here and you're making me go down memory lane!"

Just like that, it was back to work.

Eddie and I worked our abs, legs and about to start on the upper body. "Notice how all the chest machines are located in the same section? They used to label them better but I think it was hurting their trainer business. That's another reason to avoid a trainer. The gym's taking a cut. And look at the trainers here. Half of them are out of shape."

Eddie and I shared an appreciation for physical fitness and activity. Chuck liked to take Bunk for walks but that was about it. He wouldn't be caught dead in a gym. Unlike Eddie, I still ran and competed in local races. At this point, it is pure drudgery. I ran this one race, called The Old School Trail run. They didn't post a course map beforehand. It started off easy enough, on the main trail in the Wissahickon. That's completely flat. But after less than a half mile, we turned right and started going straight up. Halfway up the first hill, I was running so slow, I was barely running. I decided to walk the hills and run everywhere else. A bunch of runners would pass me going up and then I would pass them on the flats. It had to have been super annoying to the other runners.

Eddie pointed out some guy that was lifting too much weight on a curl machine. "See how his arms barely extend and his butt keeps coming up off the seat? Full range of motion. I don't get guys like that. Does he think people go around checking how much weight other people lift? It's always the older guys that do that, never the women. Women tend to lift too little weight. You see these woman lifting with a bored look on their faces and it turns out they have the machine set at five pounds."

"Did you see that there's a new Planet Fitness on Ridge?" I asked Eddie.

"I wouldn't be caught dead in that gym. What a racket. That gym's supposed to appeal to novices. You know what they're doing, don't you? They want the person that's not going to go to the gym, to join. They don't want someone like myself. Shit, they don't even have bench presses there. Then they charge ten bucks a month. Sounds like a good deal, right? That's so when you haven't used the gym for five months you'll say to yourself, *Fuck it, it's only ten bucks.*

Then they get all their gym members to clean the machines for them. There's cleaning supplies all over the place. I'm surprised they don't put mops out."

Eddie had an opinion about everything.

"Look, I have one last thing to say to you about lifting," Eddie proclaimed. "There are people who claim that if you lift too much you're going to get musclebound. Not true. You have muscles for a reason. If you don't use them, they go away. Look at your arm after you get a cast taken off. You hardly have an arm after that. Do you want your muscles to disappear? People claim that if you lift and stop, the muscle turns to fat. Bullshit! Those people are just lazy. If you want to live a long active life, get your ass in the gym and push some fucking weights."

CHAPTER 7

—◀◯▶—

I WAS WALKING PAST THE OLD EAGLE Tavern and saw Rick sitting inside at the bar. We never go to the Old Eagle, so I wondered if Rick wanted to be left alone but then thought, 'what if Rick saw me walking by and thought I didn't want to see him?' I took a step towards the bar door, then thought, 'I really don't want to drink right now' and was about to turn around when Rick looked up and caught my eye. Then I had no choice but to feign happiness, enter the bar and say hi.

"Hey man."

"Hey Declan."

"You here by yourself?"

"Yeah. I was in the neighborhood and figured what the heck. What are you up to?"

"I was just out for a walk and saw you sitting here. Thought I'd say hello."

"I guess I must look like some pathetic drunk?"

"No way! There's like a hundred bars in town. It's important to support the local economy."

"Yeah, right. It's amazing that anything gets done in this town."

"How's it going?"

"I'm hanging in there. What about you?"

"Good. No complaints. Hey, I've been meaning to ask you, have you seen Sully?"

"Sully? No, his dad died and left him a pretty nice chunk of money. Believe it or not, he moved to Maui and bought a coffee plantation."

"What?! How did I not know that?"

"He didn't really tell anyone. He just started posting pictures on Facebook and let everyone figure it out for themselves."

"I guess I have to get on Facebook."

"You don't want to do that. Can you imagine?"

"Yeah, I guess so. Everybody would start coming out of the woodwork."

The bartender came over and I felt obligated to order a beer. So much for exercise.

"How does it feel?"

"What?"

"You know. Being rich?"

Believe it or not, I was happy that my friends felt comfortable asking me that question.

"Not sure yet. It hasn't been that long. I guess, I'm still trying to get used to it."

"Seems it would be easy."

"You'd think. But before I had it, I couldn't lose it. It's like I've been given some land to protect."

"We're all afraid of something."

"That's true."

"Fucking fear."

"You sure you're okay? How's work?"

Rick was the only person I was afraid to ask about work. But it seemed inevitable. He was consumed by it. Not like some Type-A jerk off, but in the way that all his value came from his performance at work. You always knew when things were going poorly for Rick at his job. I've never known anyone that wanted success as badly but seemed unable to achieve it. He had no patience. What I knew was that Rick would have some success but then expect everything, right away. He wanted to be offered a management position. He wanted some company that he was proposing to, to be so impressed by his abilities and offer him a better job. He got those ideas because he would hear about something like that happening to someone he knew and then wondered why it hadn't happened to him. Take Sully, for instance. Sully landed a marketing position, paying close to six figures, with a law firm, when Rick and he were working inside sales. It didn't matter that two years later, Sully was back with the Phone Company. Maybe Rick thought it would have been different if it was him?

Rick was never happy for anyone. No one. Never. Didn't happen. It was always someone "lucked out" or knowing the right person. Rick might act happy for you, like the way he did with Eddie and me. Then you would hear different from a third party. After experiences like that it was really hard to remain friends with the guy.

"When you and Eddie brought in the deal with the theater chain, it hurt but I could handle it because there were always other sales to be made. I felt comfortable at work; there wasn't anyone breathing down my neck or making me report where I was or what I'd been up to. My manager knew me and treated me with respect.

"Then, gradually, things became different. We started hearing rumors. It was a little harder to close deals. Our prices seemed too high. It took the company some time to respond. But when they lowered our pricing, they didn't alter our objectives. You had to close more deals to make your numbers. But no one seemed to be making them. We lost our feeling of security. Did the company care? Did they really expect us to sell enough to make quota? Quota seemed so arbitrary.

"But they did care. My manager got pushed out and I got a new manager. The new guy had to prove himself; he brought in his own people; everything I did was questioned. We had these silly meetings where we'd take turns detailing our sales funnels. It was mostly bullshit; we were like a group of fiction writers. But there was always someone making deals the rest of us could only dream about. The managers locked onto those guys. Say you threw out an excuse, it would be, 'What about… and…? Those guys are making it.' It was hard not to question yourself."

Rick was letting it all out. It was like an orgasm of bitterness. It didn't matter if I was even there.

"I decided I couldn't take it anymore and just needed to get out; I was so happy when I got the Sales Engineer position. I could finally leave the frontline. I got my dignity back. I started to feel like a man again. I liked going to work. It felt good to team up with the sales reps, and since I had some experience there, I could help those guys, especially the young ones. I had empathy. On more than one occasion I talked up a rep on the ride back from a rough appointment. Nobody ever did that for me. The sales reps seemed to appreciate it too; many came to me directly when they needed an engineer's help.

"Then we were acquired and the new company had twice the number of sales engineers that they needed. I was given a choice, go back to sales or leave the company. I had bills to pay. Damn bills. I don't know how some people do it. You hear these stories about people that quit their jobs or were fired and they started something big and never had to work for anyone again. Or what about immigrants that can barely speak English, but they come to this country and end up owning hotels and gas stations. How do they do it?"

Didn't Rick get the memo that a job with the Phone Company had turned into more of a stepping stone than a career?

"I'm afraid to be late on one bill. That's the way I was raised. My mom paid her bills when she received them, not when they were due. I mean, what was I supposed to do? Not pay my rent? Miss a car payment? And how am I supposed to save when I'm earning a little more each month than what I owe?

"The more I try to conserve, the more sheepish I become. I'm almost forty and I've never missed a payment or defaulted on a loan but yet I'm consumed by that fear. It's like I've woken up every morning for thirty-nine years in a warm bed and I've always seen the sun but I'm afraid that it's going to end. I see dopes all around me, surviving, getting by and I'm afraid? I live next to people that I don't think have jobs but they don't seem to have a care in the world. I'm the one that's worried. But they're throwing a ton of garbage away. Garbage had to start somewhere. I mean, an empty beer bottle was full at some point, right?

"I have to man up. I tell myself to find a new job and I start looking at what's out there and I start to feel a burning in my stomach; I want to use the bathroom. Then I think, I can do it. Hang in there. I wish they'd just fire me."

I really didn't know what to say when he was through.

Rick became instantly embarrassed. It was like he snapped out of hypnosis and found himself pirouetting like a ballerina.

"I got to go," Rick said abruptly. Before I could respond, he threw a twenty on the bar and walked out.

CHAPTER 8

—◄○►—

CHUCK AND I DECIDED TO TAKE Bunk for a walk in the Wissahickon. It wasn't going to be one of our massive, two-hour walks. We planned on stopping at the park on the other side of the Walnut Street Bridge and head into one of the trails from there. That way Bunk could mix it up with some other dogs before we entered the woods.

The park we were going to, the white people brought their dogs there and the blacks barbecued. Call me racist if you want but in the few years we've been going there, I've never seen a white person barbecuing at the park and only witnessed one black guy there with a dog. If the park ranger wasn't around, you could let your dog off the leash and it could run around with the other dogs. From my experience, black people aren't big fans of dogs, especially if they're Bunk's size. Unfortunately, dogs like Bunk have a keen sense of smell and are drawn to the smell of barbecue. The result made it difficult for Chuck and me to visit the place more than once each month.

The first thing Chuck and I would do is look for the park ranger and then act accordingly. He was there so we had to keep Bunk on his leash. Same with the dozen other dog owners. We all looked like a bunch of phonies walking around with our leashed dogs. Then we saw the park ranger leave. Everyone waited an appropriate amount of time before unleashing their dogs.

There were a half a dozen regulars who were unfazed by the black - dog tension. They brought beach chairs and coolers with them and sat around drinking and talking while their dogs socialized. Chuck and I weren't part of that crowd but that didn't stop Bunk from helping himself to most of the water in a dish they set out for their dogs. Unless there was a great dane in attendance, Bunk would be the biggest dog there, so he'd act like he owned the place. He'd pee and dump wherever he wanted and devour any food or water sitting around.

"They put Rick on a performance plan," Chuck informed me.

"Really? That's explains a lot. I ran into him at The Old Eagle the other day."

"Yeah, he's been wigging out."

Nothing is worse than being placed on a performance plan if you're in sales. It's supposed to be a method to help a salesperson improve his or her performance but it's really just a way to push an underperforming sales rep out the door. Typically, the offending sales person would need to meet with his or her sales manager before and after that person's work day, to go over pending opportunities and discuss selling strategies. Frequently, there's a requirement for a certain number of cold calls completed, business cards collected, scheduled appointments, bill copy obtained and proposals delivered. All that activity should result in an increase in sales. A performance plan is as much a pain in the ass for a sales manager as it is a sales person. For most managers, enforcing a performance plan is a big hassle and instead of micro managing a sales rep, the manager will simply set a near impossible objective. Something like X amount in new sales by the end of the month. The manager and the rep both know the target is unattainable, so basically the manager is giving the rep a month to find a new job. A performance plan took what little fun there was out of sales. A sales rep went from being mostly free to do whatever he or she saw fit to being tethered like Bunk when the park ranger was around.

No matter how they're implemented or enforced, performance plans are almost never followed. Most of the time, the offending sales rep kicks a job search into high gear. Instead of pushing hard for new sales, the rep pushes for a new job before he loses the one he has. Sales managers understand that and basically make unspoken agreements with the reps. As long as a rep stays out of the way and doesn't bother the other reps, the manager will let him be. But that's if you have a decent sales manager. The real dicks act like sadists and enforce every part of the performance plan. For a prideful guy like Rick, the embarrassment of being placed on a performance plan would be equivalent to busing Eddie's and my table at a restaurant.

Rick was the only one of our group that tried to stick it out with the phone company. The rest of us had enough foresight to start looking for other opportunities before we'd ever be asked to leave. And I don't blame Rick for his struggles. There was no way he'd be able to do what was necessary to succeed at the phone company under the current circumstances. You'd have to be brand new and not know any better. A guy like Rick wouldn't be able to block out the overwhelming odds against him. Rick was a determined guy and not a quitter, even when it would have been in his best interest.

"Does he have any other prospects?" I asked Chuck.

"He could go work for one of the CLECs," Chuck replied.

A CLEC was one of the phone company's competitors. They're smaller companies and extremely sales focused. One might be willing to hire Rick because frankly, they'll hire almost anyone who has experience and shows interest and they'd hope Rick would be able to bring some of his customers with him. But businesses really don't work that way. It's highly unlikely that a business would choose to change carriers just because their account manager did. If Rick went in that direction, it would be similar to using morphine to kick a heroin addiction. He'd do it to buy himself two or three months of income. The turnover at a CLEC is very high. The sales managers there are adept at processing sales reps; they hire and fire as quickly as possible. A performance plan is written into the job description if you're selling for a CLEC.

If Rick had some money stowed away, he'd be better off starting his own business or taking his time and finding a position that would offer him a better chance to succeed. Chuck and I weren't sure if that was the case.

Chuck and I worked our way through the park area and past the smoking barbecues and down into the Wissahickon. We headed down a steep trail, over a little bridge, along a wooded ridge, across some concrete pipes, stopped and watched Bunk bathe in and drink from a small pool of water, went through a rock formation, walked down some flat rocks configured into a trail staircase until we reached our destination, a larger pool of water at the base of the park. Along the way, Chuck would need to proclaim that Bunk was a friendly dog to any of the oncoming dog walkers. The men would be cool but the women were almost always over protective of their dogs. Bunk never started anything but would definitely fight back, and it was the smaller dogs that were the most aggressive.

Bunk was just big and made people uncomfortable. "He's friendly" replaced "Hello" or "Good morning." Britt got so used to saying it, she said it to an approaching couple when she was walking by herself, one day.

The park was magnificent in the fall. The leaves were turning and fell from the trees like giant, colorful snowflakes. The air was dry and cool. The sun burst through the less dense foliage. Leaf rustling added another dimension to our footsteps.

When we reached the water, Bunk would sink himself in but he wouldn't swim. It didn't matter if it was ninety or ten degrees, Bunk would enter the water either way. It made us wonder how hot he must feel on a warm day. Our walks in the park were probably the most peaceful time in our lives. We were exercising; we weren't eating unhealthy food, spending money or getting into trouble and wouldn't be hung over the next day. As much as we enjoyed the park, Bunk was in heaven. He chased squirrels and would leap in the air and pound the ground with his front paws, in an attempt to scare the chipmunks out of their hiding places. If we stumbled upon some deer, Bunk would be off in pursuit. He might disappear for fifteen minutes or more. He'd return without any indication of success, happy and exhausted.

CHAPTER 9

―◁○▷―

C HUCK'S GRANDMA IS NINETY-TWO. SHE LIVES outside of Philadelphia, in a Main Line neighborhood where the yards are huge and the houses are routinely demolished and replaced with mcmansions. Grandma Cooley has lived in her house for over fifty years. Despite her age, she attends to all the gardens surrounding her home. Chuck and I have stopped by to discover two trash cans full of weeds and grass that she pulled herself. Chuck's grandma says her yard is her gym. The yard work keeps her young, or as young as a ninety-two year old could ever be.

Chuck's grandma volunteered at a nearby hospital thrift store, but not necessarily because she was altruistic. Mostly she volunteered there because she was able to sift through the donations and pick out items she liked and then assign an agreeable price. Chuck told me that one church morning his grandma showed off some new shoes she purchased at the thrift store for five dollars. During the ceremony, the soles of the shoes disintegrated; there was sole particles all over the carpet where she was standing. You'd think, since Grandma Cooley wasn't hurting financially and the thrift store was a method for the hospital to raise funds that she would have written off the defective shoe money. But no, she accepted a full refund.

Grandma Cooley's favorite actor, in fact the only actor she has ever spoken about, according to Chuck, is Dustin Hoffman. That might be the case because Mrs. Cooley and Mr. Hoffman look like they could be age different twins.

Mrs. Cooley has noticeably large hands. Chuck thinks they're larger than his own; they surprise him every time he holds one. Chuck believes it's the result of all her yard work.

Grandma Cooley is shrinking. I've known her for ten years and she seems to be half the size she was when we first met.

Chuck and I stop by her house whenever we're in the neighborhood. The side door we enter is made out of wood, swells in the humidity and can be difficult to open. Grandpa Cooley installed a metal plate at the base of the door, to protect the wood, because everyone made a habit of kicking it open. Despite the door kicking, Grandma Cooley never hears us entering her home. We've journeyed all the way to the fourth floor of the split level home looking for her and still Chuck will need to tap a shoulder to get her attention. We dislike the exercise because we're afraid that at some point we'll startle her for the last time.

I liked it better when Chuck brings Bunk with him. That way Bunk could go on ahead and sniff out Mrs. Cooley for us. Then she knows were in the house. She liked Bunk, even after the time he went after a squirrel when she had his leash wrapped around one of her fingers. Chuck lost a dog sitter and Grandma Cooley almost lost a finger.

Grandma Cooley naps on her back with her mouth wide open. Chuck hates to find her that way. He told me he watches her chest to see if it's moving before making his approach.

"Let me get my hearing aid" is the first thing Grandma Cooley will say after you startle her. The second thing is, "Can you…?" Grandma Cooley is reliant on others to perform a number of tasks and obsesses about them until they're completed. She won't write them down and as soon as she sees someone, the requests blurt out of her mouth like water from an unkinked hose.

Grandma Cooley is a voracious reader. When she's not reading a book, she's reading the subtitles on her TV screen. After she unleashes her task demands, she'll discharge a stream of information that she accumulated between visitors.

Grandpa Cooley died two years ago. They were married for over sixty years. Chuck's been a big comfort to his grandma. He helps her with the yard and even takes her to church. He's not a believer, though. The item that drowned his faith was hearing his grandma's church's version of Exodus 20:17, "Thou shalt not covet thy neighbor's house, wife, slave, ox or any other of his possessions. That is the word of the lord." To Chuck that meant that either God was pro slavery and considered a man's wife a possession and equivalent to any of his other belongings, or it was all bull. It had to be one or the other. It was amazing Chuck even heard the reading because most of the time at church, he's completely zoned out and has his mind on other things.

"Oh, I see you've brought Declan with you. Hi Declan," Grandma Cooley said and gave me a sly look and bright smile. *Is Grandma Cooley flirting with me?*

"Charles, before you leave, could you go upstairs and hang the plant in my bedroom? I can't reach that high." Chuck's grandma calls him "Charles" which makes us laugh. "Also, I want to put the wheelbarrow in the garage, up in the shed." Chuck understood that what his Grandma wanted should be what he wanted too.

"When I'm finished reading this book, I want you to read it," Mrs. Cooley said to Chuck. Chuck didn't share his grandma's interest but it was easier to agree because she'd make the same offer to five other people, and someone would take her up on it.

"Are you going to stay for lunch?"

There were three things Grandma Cooley adhered to, breakfast, lunch and dinner. Noon was lunch time with absolutely no flexibility. Six-thirty was dinner. A common topic during meals was the planning of other meals and what to do with excess food. Grandma Cooley was very concerned about surplus food. "Charles, can you finish the noodles? Declan, would you like to take some meatloaf home with you?" If you agreed to take food with you, Grandma Cooley would place it in an old piece of Tupperware with a missing lid. She'd then use an odd cover that didn't fit. So she had to fasten the lid with a rubber band, but that wouldn't seal completely so she'd place the random basin with the misfitting cover into a ziplock bag that either wouldn't seal or she didn't have the patience for because she used a second rubber band to keep the bag closed. Despite her heavy food management, her refrigerator was packed. If Chuck and I were over and brought a six pack to share, we'd have to split it up to get the bottles to fit. We started bringing a cooler with ice. And it wasn't like Mrs. Cooley owned a small fridge. She had a brand new one, with double doors and a large freezer underneath.

It's important to check the date before you eat anything out of Grandma Cooley's fridge. Chuck once found a two-year old yogurt in there.

All the meals at Mrs. Cooley's house are handmade. Our only hope was that she washed before she maneuvered our food with her oversized hands.

Along with the freezer that came with her fridge, Mrs. Cooley has another bigger freezer in her garage. The freezer was a bone of contention between Chuck and his grandma. He says that she adds two extra steps to the cooking process, freezing and thawing. Mrs. Cooley must have lived in a time when you couldn't go to the grocery store any day of the week and pick up a flank steak, because she buys them two weeks ahead of time. "Charles, can you come to dinner next Saturday? The Wilsons are coming and it helps to have you there to entertain. I bought a flank steak to prepare."

Chucks ribs his grandma about her use of the freezer. When her old freezer died he contested her purchase of a replacement. The same woman that wouldn't purchase a color TV, a clothes dryer or install central air until the late eighties, was willing to pay five hundred dollars for a new freezer. If you walk around Grandma Cooley's house and look on the back of a picture or on the underside of a piece of furniture, you'll find a yellow sticky with Chuck's or one of his sisters' names on it. That's how they decided to divvy up everything when their grandma passes. Grandma Cooley attached a note to the front of her new freezer, "This freezer goes to my grandson, Charles."

Chuck emails his grandma almost every day. They've been emailing each other since the days of dialup. He's shown me a few of her emails. It seems that she has forgone proofreading, capitalization, most punctuation and correct spelling. One time Chuck mentioned that Britt's family would like it if he relocated to Princeton. Chuck could work from almost anywhere and Britt wishes she lived closer. "you can tel them that they can stick princetn up ther asses," was Grandma Cooley's reply.

Grandma Cooley made us grilled cheese and ham sandwiches. She was getting better in the kitchen. Grandpa Cooley did all the cooking before he died, even when he was connected to an oxygen tank. Fortunately, the Cooley's didn't own a gas stove.

We ate in the dining room. Every square inch of her house was decorated in one way or another. Mrs. Cooley was an artist and you could tell. "I just painted some flowers in a vase. I think it's my best work." She was something. Every birthday, Chuck received a hand painted card and every time he moved, a hand painted house sign.

"It's okay if you can't take me to church this Sunday. I can bring my cane," Mrs. Cooley informed Chuck.

"You have two grandsons that take you to church, Cane and Able," Chuck quipped.

"Good one Abel," I muttered.

After we were done with lunch, Chuck and I had to be on our way. Mrs. Cooley didn't mind, she was happy when we dropped in and when we left. Chuck gave her a nice hug. "Love you grandma."

"Oh, thank you," Grandma Cooley replied.

If you're wondering what Chuck's dad's involvement was, he was no longer around. It's a topic that was totally off limit. Even Eddie knows not to go there.

CHAPTER 10

---◄○►---

CHUCK'S DAD WAS THE SMARTEST PERSON Chuck ever knew, including me, and he was ten times more disciplined. In 1999, Napster brought the technology of file sharing to the forefront. At that point, it was limited to MP3 files, mostly due to the lack of available internet bandwidth.

In 1999, Chuck's dad was a forty-four year old technician working in research and development for Unisys Corporation. He made a comfortable living; Chuck's family lived in a nice home near the Valley Forge National Park; all of Chuck's five siblings were expected to attend college; Chuck's mom was a stay at home mother and full time political thorn in the side of the area Republicans.

A funny thing can happen to a man when he's approaching his fifties and hasn't left his stamp on the world. Some men lose it and start working out, have an affair with a younger woman, divorce their wives and annoy the hell out of their kids. Chuck's dad didn't do that. He dove headfirst into internet technology and spent every waking, non-working hour to develop a new innovation.

Every "non-working hour" was stretching the truth, because Chuck's dad was in R&D and wasn't closely monitored. He could make it appear he was working on company projects when that wasn't always the case.

About this time, Chuck was attending college at Drexel University. He had five younger sisters, between the ages of nine and seventeen. His mom would complain to Chuck, during their visits and phone calls, about Chuck's dad being holed up in their basement working on his computer. Chuck's dad barely made time for his children or wife. He only came upstairs to grab some food or coffee and then it was back down. He ended up installing a small fridge and coffee maker downstairs, so he wouldn't have to waste time walking back and forth between the basement and the kitchen. This went on for about a year. Then he installed a lock on the basement door and started sleeping down there. The only time his family saw him was before he showered (which was becoming less frequent) and on his way out the door to go to work.

When Chuck's mom tried talking to her husband, he listened patiently but never altered his routine. He was earning a living; he wasn't involved in anything illegal or salacious, so Chuck's mom was willing to let him be. She figured he had to do what he was doing, in order to get it out of his system. What was her choice? She could try to make him stop but she knew how determined he was. He had always been a loving and devoted husband; up until this point in his life, he was everything she ever wished for.

Down in the basement, Chuck's dad taught himself how to write code. He learned Python, JavaScript and HTML. Chuck's dad was accomplishing some pretty amazing things without really being aware of what they were because he kept it to himself. These were the days before the popularity of Google and Facebook, so information wasn't as omnipresent as it is today. Had Chuck's dad been working with anyone he would have been more aware of what was going on in the world around him, specifically on the west coast. He just plugged away, day after day, energized by the virtual world of internet technology.

Months and years passed by. Chuck's family grew accustomed to their father's habits. At this point he was living fulltime in the basement. He installed a shower and an outside entrance. Most every other woman would have filed for divorce, but Chuck's mom remained devoted. Chuck and two of his sisters were attending college. Her other three children were headed in that direction. If Chuck's mom threw a fit, what would that accomplish? Any sort of separation or divorce proceeding, could jeopardize the kid's college funds.

In the early 2000's digital cameras were in their infancy, so there was little video content being generated by the general populace. It wasn't until cameras became commonplace on mobile phones before people started filming everything imaginable and looking for a way to share it. Chuck's dad was something of a visionary because he saw how the technologies would merge. Later on, Chuck would browse through the many journals his father kept and see crude sketches of people aiming tiny devices at their kids' sporting events.

Chuck's dad didn't quit his job because he didn't want to lose the income. He also didn't inform anyone what he was up to because he didn't want his coworkers discussing the project or looking over his shoulder. He completed just enough work to stay employed and hoped that his reputation would be enough to bridge the gap between his current employment and experiencing the payoff from his efforts in the basement. When he wasn't at work, he was down there and the only people he communicated with from down there were on forums and in chat rooms and Chuck's dad was tight lipped because he didn't want to reveal his big idea.

After four years in the basement, Chuck's dad was more than crazy. He might have been close to inventing a program that would revolutionize the way people shared video but he was in no condition to manage a company or talk to investors. Chuck, on the other hand, was busy doing his own thing. He was trying to prepare himself for a life after college. He was thinking about girls and partying with his friends. When he was home, he was busy being the man of the house. At that point, Chuck hated his dad. He was embarrassed by his behavior. Most of Chuck's friends assumed he didn't have a dad because he never came around and Chuck never spoke of him.

There is a phenomenon referred to as simultaneous invention or multiple discovery. That's when different people or groups experience a similar breakthrough or discovery, at or about the same time. It happens more often than you'd think. The reason you don't hear about it that often because all the focus goes to the first person or group that goes public.

While Chuck's dad was busy in the basement, three guys who helped develop PayPal were about to strike gold once again on another effort called YouTube.

A year before YouTube went public, Chuck's dad's site was mostly completed. Problem was Chuck's dad was a perfectionist. He kept tweaking and tweaking his program. He wanted it to be perfect before he'd ever consider showing it to anyone. At one point, he totally rebuilt the site because he didn't like the way it appeared on the new Apple computer he brought home.

In December of 2004, Chuck's dad felt he was close enough to quit his job. He didn't bother to inform his wife of the decision. Chuck's mom hoped he was using up vacation days when she noticed he wasn't leaving for work in the morning. Christmas and New Year's came and went with the family celebrating without their father. Chuck's mom experienced another Valentine's Day without so much as a hello from her husband. At this point, she was nearing her limit, which was way past what most women would have put up with.

Valentine's Day that year was more brutal to Chuck's dad than it was to his mother. It was on that day that YouTube was introduced. The same day that press releases were circulating that information, Chuck's father was putting the finishing touches on his program. It was almost ready to be unveiled. It took another few months for him to learn about the existence of YouTube. One day, he had to visit his old place of employment to sign some documents and retrieve some items. He was walking past an ex coworker's cubicle when something captured his attention. That person was watching a video of two pandas playing in a tree. Chuck's dad stopped in his tracks. He entered the stranger's cubicle and demanded to know what he was looking at.

"You haven't seen this? They're two pandas from the San Diego Zoo. So funny."

"I don't mean the video itself, what program is that?"

"Oh, it's this new website called YouTube. You should check it out."

It was unknown what the weight of this discovery felt like to Chuck's dad because he never confided with anyone. It was a story in passing, after the fact that lead to this information. Chuck's dad learned that the project he'd been obsessing about for the last five years was already in place, and it was developed by people with many more connections than he would ever possess. Chuck's dad had quit his job at the age of fifty, with a handful of kids to put through college and a wife that hadn't worked in years.

The story of Chuck's dad's obsession was pieced together by Chuck. He did so by reading through dozens of his father's journals and reviewing the files saved on his computer. According to Chuck, his dad's program had some advantages over YouTube. For instance, his program offered slow motion viewing and multiple screen sizes. But Chuck also realized that towards the end his dad had lost his mind. His dad was sure that the government was spying on him. The real reason he quit his job was so he could guard his computer around the clock. He was considering reinforcing the basement walls so they could withstand an air strike. Maybe the most frightening item that Chuck discovered were the notes he kept about his family.

In one of his father's journal entries, he read that it was Chuck that he distrusted the most. His father was sure that Chuck would come down to the basement at night, when he was asleep, to view his files and steal his work. To prevent that from happening Chuck's dad moved the couch up against his computer every night. That way Chuck couldn't access his computer without stirring him.

Chuck's dad referred to his wife and daughters as "bitches" and "cunts". The entire time that his wife was giving him space and trying not interfere, Chuck's dad was resentful of her. It was her fault that he hadn't achieved more. He was going to show them all and then be done with them.

He had written out scripts for the talk shows he expected to be booked on. One "interview" he did with Larry King was ten pages long. A couple pages later he sketched himself on the cover of Time Magazine.

After Chuck's father discovered YouTube, his journals took a one hundred and eighty degree turn. He was full of remorse. There were pages where the ink had run. Chuck's conclusion that it had to be from his father's tears. On another page he wrote the word "stupid" over and over again, each time with more force. Towards the end of the page the writing was so hard it tore the paper. Chuck paged ahead a dozen pages and could still see the impression of the word.

I'm the only person other than Chuck, and I assume Britt, that know about the journals. Chuck kept them from his mother and siblings. They had been through enough.

His father's last journal entry was:

"It's over."

That was it.

Chuck's father did his best to disguise his intentions. He didn't leave a note or tip off anyone. Chuck figures he must have driven for hours to find the right set of circumstances. He ended up driving his car into the backside of semi-truck with no rear t-bumper. His dad's car ended up three quarters of its length under the truck before it stopped completely. It was a gruesome scene for those who witnessed it.

Chuck's father had a one-million dollar life insurance policy with a double indemnity provision. If his father suffered an accidental death, his mother would receive two times the death benefit. Chuck's mom ended up with two million dollars to put towards her family's future. It was the only way Chuck's father could think of to repay his family for what he had done to them. In a way, due to his time in the basement, they were better prepared for his passing.

Chuck's dad passed and a year after it was unveiled, YouTube was purchased by Google for 1.65 billion dollars.

CHAPTER 11

◄─○─►

EVERYONE MET AT CHUCK'S HOUSE TO watch the Eagles – Cowboys game. Chuck didn't have the best TV so I wasn't sure why we were watching it at his place. Most likely it was because Britt would be home and cooking.

Chuck resides in the strangest place in Manayunk. He lives in a row of houses that are right off the train tracks. To get to his house, you either had to drive down a hidden road that ran along the tracks, past Henkel Roofing, or park near Dawson's and walk across a bridge, over the same tracks. Literally, Chuck could trip walking out his front door and tumble in front of an oncoming train. His group of houses must have been built for railroad workers; they wouldn't be any closer to the tracks if they originated from a converted railroad station.

The reason why Chuck loved the place was his back patio. He had an amazing view of the Schuylkill River, the Schuylkill Expressway and almost everything else named Schuylkill. Chuck loved to sit back there, drink beer and listen to his iTunes.

Everybody was there that day: Rick, me, John and even Eddie. Chuck wouldn't normally invite Eddie but I insisted. Chuck gets a little put off by Eddie's cutting wit. I don't think Eddie can help it. He's lightning quick and words fly out of his mouth before he has a chance to think about what he's saying. Eddie also grew up listening to Howard Stern and sometimes forgets that he's not on the show and not everyone is a fan of constant ballbusting.

"Nice TV. Where did you get it from, a museum?" Eddie asked when he walked in, immediately ingratiating himself to the host.

Eddie can't stop himself. He knows he can get on people's nerves but at least every third thing he says is very funny. Eddie lives for those moments and when he tries to censor himself he becomes a little boring.

Chuck sat in the master's chair; a recliner that had become an extension of Chuck's bony bod. Eddie and I got the couch. John and Rick, since they were last to arrive, sat in table chairs, temporarily stationed on either side of the couch. Britt didn't need a chair; she'd be buzzing around the room taking care of our every request.

It was in those times when Chuck felt like the man. Britt adored him and pretty much set the benchmark for women for the rest of us.

I brought a case of Yards. We used to drink Yuengling until they started brewing it in Tampa, Florida. Then it began to taste like piss. Britt whipped up an assortment of finger foods. I never had anything she made that didn't make me pause. I can cook but I can also sing, and no one would ever want to listen to me. When I eat the food I prepare, it seems fine. It wasn't until I started eating Britt's dishes that I understood that there was a substantial difference.

Dallas is the most hated team in Philadelphia. You don't even have to say "Cowboys" because no one would consider the Mavericks or the Stars if you used "Dallas" in a sentence pertaining to sports in

Philadelphia. The Mets, Lakers, Giants and Redskins are also hated but with nowhere near the venom that the Cowboys produce.

Eddie's joke, "My two favorite teams are the Eagles and whatever team is playing the Cowboys" even makes Chuck laugh.

If the Eagles only won two games the whole season and those two were against the Cowboys, most Philadelphians would be okay with that.

Why do we hate the Cowboys? Because the Cowboys attract the worst type of fan base imaginable. The Raiders are a close second, with their pseudo violent, costume wearing following but to Philadelphians, Cowboy fans are the most objectionable.

Before I explain why, I have to explain Philadelphians. Philadelphians are taught early on the importance of rooting for the home team and that sports are more important than just about anything else in life. With the crappy weather, dirty streets, horrible traffic… sports provide the average Philadelphian a place to escape.

Philly people love to bitch about their teams. They don't know what to do with themselves when one of them wins a championship. Also, the athlete that will receive the most criticism is the best player on one of their teams. Just ask Mike Schmidt. He is arguably the best third baseman that ever played and was booed more often at home than on the road. Charles Barkley was one of the best power forwards to ever play in the NBA but Philadelphia fans labeled him a cancer and couldn't wait for the team to get rid of him. The Sixers traded Barkley to the Suns for two nickels and a dime. The Suns went to the finals the following year; the Sixers didn't reach the playoffs.

The Eagles are Philadelphia's number one team. That's because football is the city's favorite sport but also probably because the Eagles have never won the Super Bowl.

So what is it that Philadelphians find so objectionable about Cowboy fans? If Dallas were a more regional team, meaning their fan base was more centrally located, there wouldn't be a problem. The Cowboy fans that people from Philly hate are the ones that never lived or even been to Dallas, who started following the team during one of their winning eras. Frontrunners. Nothing is more objectionable than someone growing up in Philly and making the Cowboys his favorite team. I say "his" because only guys exhibit this dickish behavior. Women seem to know better. The fact that there is a Cowboy's section in a local Modell's makes me not want to shop there.

Ask any one of these fair weather fans how his fandom originated and he will always say he's been a fan since, and then mention some old time Cowboys' player in an attempt to justify his treacherous behavior.

Everyone in Chuck's house was an Eagles fan. There's no way we'd be able to sit through the game with someone from the opposing team in attendance. It was a bright, sunny October day. It wasn't jacket weather but you might want to double up on top.

The Eagles experienced a quick three and out and Rick was ready to give up on them. There's always one of those in the crowd; the kind of person that wants to throw in the towel early. I think they do it to lower their expectations. If they start out thinking that their team is going to lose and it wins – bonus. If their team loses – they got a head start in the grieving process.

"These sliders are amazing, Britt!" John exclaimed. "I wish my wife could cook like you."

I'm sure John's wife would be happy to hear that.

"My mother's church is ridiculous," Eddie asserted.

"Why's that?" Rick asked.

"They scheduled a fundraising picnic for today, right during the game. You'd think they'd know the Eagles' schedule. No one is going to go. Everyone's going to want to be home watching the game."

"Maybe they scheduled it that way for a reason?" I offered.

"What do you mean?"

"You're right; no one will want to miss the game. But you mentioned that it was a fundraiser. So all the men and women that want to skip the picnic, they'll donate money instead. The church knows the attendance will be low so they can skimp on picnic supplies."

"Bet you didn't consider that Eddie," Chuck chimed in.

"Bet you haven't bought a new TV in ten years," Eddie fired back.

Another missed first down and another Eagles punt added to the tension building in the room.

"I like the Yards Pale Ale, but have you tasted the ESA? It's like twice the strength for the same price. You can really save by drinking stronger beer." John offered.

"The IPA is even stronger," Chuck replied.

"I know but a little too bitter for my taste." John responded.

"You have to drink it really cold. I turn up the refrigerator and store my glasses in the freezer. Everything else in the fridge freezes but at least my beer is cold," Chuck offered.

"I'm sure Britt loves that," I asserted.

"Ever notice how warm the draft beer is in Manayunk? You cannot get a cold glass of beer at any bar around here. The only way to get cold beer is if you order it in bottles," Eddie proclaimed.

"I have noticed that. Is it because they store the kegs in the basement?" Rick asked.

"If anything it would be cooler in the basement. Heat rises," Chuck stated.

"Nothing's more disappointing than to walk into a bar on a hot day, order a draft and take a gulp of beer that's just a bit cooler than the air temperature. And I prefer draft," Eddie said.

"Beer's beer. It doesn't matter if it comes from a bottle or a keg. Just pour the bottle in a glass," John proclaimed.

Having John around sometimes felt like hanging out with your dad. We loved him but he made a habit of shutting down our nonsensical conversations.

After a near altercation between him and Eddie, John became our favorite installer at the Phone Company. If John was on the job it was going to get done right.

"The carrots are frozen!" we could hear Britt bellow from the kitchen.

"It's amazing how much beer has changed. There are so many varieties available now. Remember when it was just Bud, Miller and Coors?" Rick asked.

"It drives me crazy when you are at a place with so many great beer choices and some jerk off orders a Miller Lite," Eddie contributed.

"Have you guys been to Wegmans?" John asked.

"A couple of times," Rick replied. Everyone else mumbled a response.

"It's great that you can buy beer there but what the...? I go there and I put a couple of six packs in my cart and then went through the rest of the store to pick up some other items my wife said we needed. I go to checkout and they tell me I can't pay for the beer in the grocery checkout; I have to buy it in the beer checkout. Next time I'm in the store, I think, okay we need some corn chips and orange juice, I'll get those items first and pay for everything at the beer checkout. But the woman there tells me I can't pay for groceries in the beer aisle, and I was buying too much beer and I only was trying to purchase like four six packs.

It's Pennsylvania. Do you think the legislatures had a conversation about how they'd let Wegmans sell beer and they came up with that shit?"

"You know you can buy beer, wine and liquor in a grocery store in Phoenix? Hell, you can buy a fifth of whisky at Circle K," I chipped in.

"Look, no one here knows what the hell you're talking about. Circle fucking K! You're from Philly. We shop at Wawa. If it's so great in Arizona, I'm sure they got room for you there. Go, go be a Cardinals fan. At least we root for a real bird." Eddie proclaimed as the rest of them howled.

"Okay, okay! But maybe you guys should venture out of Pennsylvania once in a while? You might learn something." I shot back.

"We've got everything we need write here, thank you very much," John contributed.

Eddie pretty much summed it up for the rest of the group. That was Philly for you. Bitch all you want but don't mention a better way.

Another possession, another Eagles punt. "Donnie Jones looks good today," Eddie remarked.

Chuck's dog Bunk entered the room. He'd been sleeping in the other room. Bunk was the most chill dog on the planet. He was some sort of shepherd mix, a hundred pounds and tall. Chuck claimed he trained Bunk to be that way. I think it's because Chuck and Britt walk him often. Anyone that spends any time around old Bunk wants to buy a dog.

"Hey Bunky!" Eddie called out. "Great dog, man. Makes me want to get one."

"You can thank me," Chuck proclaimed.

"Come on! That dog was born that way. Right Bunker?"

I think Eddie was more in love with Bunk than Chuck was.

Bunk has the scariest bark. If you were on the other side of Chuck's front door and didn't know any better, you'd think there was a killer inside. But Chuck tells me that Bunk hides in the bathroom, shaking during a thunderstorm.

Chuck had two cats, as well, Howard and Robin, named after Howard Stern and his sidekick, Robin Quivers. Robin was the black cat. Howard was gray. They were more like dogs than your typical cats. They'd go right up to a stranger and say hello. Chuck told me that Robin is especially fond of his black visitors. The phone tech that set up his services was black and Chuck had to shut Robin in a bedroom so the guy could complete his work.

Britt peaked her head in the room to ask if anyone needed a refill. Everyone smiled. She was infectious.

The first quarter ended: Eagles zero, Cowboys zero. The game was a punting contest so far.

According to Chuck, Britt refers to herself as a "chub". She's a little more than chubby but she has a beautiful face (Britt calls it her stunner) and long black hair. Her body is proportional, so she has that going for her. She's a butt man's Mona Lisa. When she bends over, she could pick a dime off the floor without flexing her knees. If you happen to witness that sight it's something you won't soon forget. I've seen her bent over looking into the refrigerator and all I could see was her butt.

Chuck has issues with Britt's weight; he wants her to exercise more and eat less, but they're very much in love. Chuck's no walk in the park. Look at where he lives, and he thinks it's the greatest place in the world.

Second quarter was underway and still more punts.

"What if the whole game was just punt returns. Two teams would take turns punting the ball until one of them ran one back. That would be exciting," Rick offered.

"I'd watch that," John replied.

"Why do we hate the Cowboys so much?" Rick asked.

"It's their fans. Every jerk off in the neighborhood made the Cowboys their favorite team." Eddie proclaimed.

"I lived near these two twin brothers, the Chias, growing up," John said. "They used to sit on either side of me at lunch and talk to me with their mouths full of egg salad. Man, egg salad disgusts me. I don't know how anyone could eat it. Anyway, they liked the Cowboys. Grew up in Philly and rooted for the Cowboys. If my kid did that I'd throw em out of the house."

"Didn't you root for the Rams when you were a kid, John?" Eddie revealed.

"That's because my dad lived in LA and followed the Rams. Their yellow and blue uniforms from the eighties were a thing of beauty."

John was very opinionated about team uniforms.

"I wised up. Fuck the Rams and fuck the Cowboys. There, you happy?"

We felt better.

"My kid got me listening to Panda," John started.

"Panda?" Eddie asked.

"You know, the music service? You enter what bands you like and it develops a custom playlist?" John replied. "You guys make fun of me for not keeping up with technology... Eddie over here never heard of Panda?"

"It's Pandora, idiot!" Eddie fired back. We all laughed.

"Oh, anyway. I heard this commercial for some swiss cheese company on there. It boasted how they only use milk from Swiss cows to make their cheese. You know, say what you want about various *ethnic* groups in this country but there's nothing wrong with our livestock!"

We all let John's assertion sink in as the game returned from a commercial break.

"Which reminds me of something. Why is steak so expensive?"

"Yeah, it's freaking crazy," Rick chimed in. "Regular strip steak is like eight bucks a pound!"

"I've driven out west, past cattle ranches and believe me, there's no shortage of cows," John asserted.

"What color were they?" Chuck asked.

"Black and white. What else?"

"Those were dairy cows," Chuck pointed out.

"So?" John asked.

"They don't slaughter dairy cows for steak meat," Chuck answered.

"Look at the cow expert over here," John replied.

"Chuck is starting to sound like a cowgirls fan," Eddie proclaimed. Even Chuck laughed.

The Cowboys broke the scoreless tie with a field goal. It was three nothing Cowboys. It was going to be stressful game to watch. We'd prefer that these games be blowouts so we could sit back, relax and make fun of Dallas, the Cowboys, the cheerleaders, their fans... If the Eagles could come out with knives and murder all the Cowboys players in the first minutes, we'd be okay with that.

"Why do they even have a two-minute warning in the first half? The game's not close to over. What are they being warned about?" Chucked asked.

More food for thought. No one bothered to reply.

The game reached halftime. We just witnessed the Eagles punt the ball seven times and miss a field goal. "If I wanted to watch soccer, I'd move to London," was Eddie's summary of the first half. We needed to get up and move around but it's not like we could go outside and toss a ball on the tracks. There's a huge difference between screaming "car" and "train!"

We decided to walk over to Dawson's to see what the crowd was like. John had enough and went home. John was always going home. We were surprised when he went out in the first place.

There was a bunch of people congregated outside the bar, a quarter of them we're smoking. Everyone was wearing various levels of fan gear. Mostly it was just jerseys and shirts. Some guys were wearing hats as well. One douche was wearing an Emmitt Smith jersey. "Asshole!" Eddie summed up what the rest of us were thinking. Some of the women were wearing pink Eagles' jerseys. If you ask me, the reason Philadelphia regularly leads the NFL in jersey sales is that a lot of the women in town buy them. Go to Modell's and check out the women's fan section; it's three times the size of the Cowboy's section.

Eddie had been texting all day. Text messaging had definitely made things easier for him. Eddie preferred it because he didn't like the way his voice sounded.

Eddie was a work in progress. He kept working on his looks because he wasn't that attractive in high school. Guys that were good looking in high school tend to let themselves go later on in life and still think they're hot shit. Guys like Eddie are always trying to improve themselves. That's probably why Eddie is such a hound.

Chuck and Rick entered the bar. Eddie and I decided to hang outside.

"You've been really going at it with the texts. Who is it this time?" I asked.

"Just some girl."

"Oh yeah, 'just some girl'?"

"I met her online. We're in the texting stage."

"There are stages?"

"You want to know how it works?"

"I have a good idea, but would like to hear your perspective."

"I'll break it down for you. There are a bunch of different sites to use. I'm cheap so I use a free one. You put up a profile. You want to use your best photos. To be quite honest, mine are getting a little long in the tooth. I'm not the most photogenic guy so when I take a decent picture, I hold on to it.

"You have to say what you're looking for and what you like to do. Now, you have to be careful. If you mark down that you're looking for a relationship, you're going to get the crazies. But if you use 'Just Want to Date' some girls will block you. I'm not really looking for a relationship but if I met Eva Mendes online, I would be ready to settle down."

"That's understandable."

"So I use 'Looking for a Relationship'. You enter an income level. I overstate mine by about twenty grand. I chose 'Ambitious' but not 'Very Ambitious' because I don't want to scare a girl. Believe it or not they have a spot where you indicate if you own a car or not."

"That's important."

"Now, I don't really send notes to girls. I let them approach me. I do drop hints like making a girl a favorite or indicating that I would like to meet them. They have this whole Meet Me feature that takes you through one girl's picture after another: Yes, No, Yes, No... Honestly, sometimes you have to plow through a whole bunch of No's before you can find a Yes.

"You have to stay away from the really hot girls. They get so much attention, it's not worth your time. You know what I like. I look for the girls with a little extra up top but sometimes you have to really study their photos to determine what they got going there."

"You know, if you put this much attention in anything else..." I stopped myself. Why bother. This was Eddie's thing.

Eddie kept going.

"When a girl I like messages me, that's just the beginning. You have to remind yourself that dozens of guys are messaging these women. That's one of the reasons I don't. But if you write something stupid and she has a bunch of other guys writing her, it's nothing for her to give up on you."

"Who knew it was so complicated?"

"Brother, let me tell you. You can't be too forward in the beginning. And you want to make sure you read the girl's profile thoroughly. Women want to be heard. If a girl took the time to write a couple paragraphs, you better not be asking her a question when the answer is buried in her profile. Oh, that reminds me. Girls to avoid: Any girl with a very lengthy profile. You'd think some of them wanted to be published. Girls with kids in their photos. Not that I'm against kids but sure don't want to date a woman that would put her kid's photo on a cheap dating site. Girls that pose with their friends. There's a bunch of unattractive women that always seem to have attractive friends. You don't know who's the friend and who's the girl. You can't ask and the last thing you want to do is plan a date and find out it's the ugly one.

Once you've traded a number of messages and the girl seems cool. You write something like, 'I don't like being on this site but I don't get out much and it seems to be the only way I can meet someone. Can we text instead?' A girl will like that because it sounds like you met her by chance and you're not trolling the internet looking for tail."

"That wouldn't be good."

"Once you start texting you're halfway home. If you're not sure about a girl and don't want to waste a lot of time with her, you might get a little frisky on text. You'd be amazed at what I can get a girl to send me."

"Oh yeah?"

"Fuck yeah. If you're any good at writing it's not too hard to get these girls eating out your hands.

"If I like a girl. I try to set up a meeting pretty quickly, before I fuck it up."

"How long have you been doing it?"

"About two years. I tell you, in the last twelve months or so, I've been with twenty-five women."

"Been with?"

"I only count intercourse. If a girl only gives me head, I don't count it."

"You're fucking with me!"

"No way dude. Let me tell you, it hasn't been a walk in the park. I had to put up with a lot of shit along the way. I mean, I had to deal with a ton of rejection and bad dates. Chicks that are much older than their photos...

"I met this one girl. She had to be fifteen years older than her photos and twenty-five pounds heavier. We met up at a bookstore. When I first saw her I wanted to walk out, pretend I was someone else. Then I thought, I'll just be nice, sit with her a bit and thank her and say goodnight. I mean, I know how it feels when someone doesn't like you. She had gotten one of those postcard books off the shelf. You know, the ones where people write down their confessions? She wanted us to sit down and go through it together. I hate those books. Fuck! So I said, 'Let's just talk.' So maybe we're sitting there for two more minutes and you know what she did?"

"What?"

"She got up and just walked out on me! She made a preemptive strike. I got rejected by someone I was going to reject. Bitch!"

"Eddie man, don't you want to meet someone special, some way more naturally?"

"Normally I would say yes. But I think I got myself hooked on some sick shit. I'm like a guy that went from pot to heroin."

"Do they have dating site rehabs?"

"Don't know. Maybe I got to go be a monk somewhere?"

"Half time's got to be over. Let's go find Chuck and Rick."

Eddie and I entered the bar and spotted Chuck and Rick talking to some girls sitting at a table.

"Hey Declan! Get over here." Chuck shouted my way.

"What's up?" I replied.

"Meet Kristy and Jennifer."

"It's Julia!" Julia corrected him.

"Sorry. Kristy and JULIA, this is my good friend Declan. He's rich." He whispered the last part.

"I'm Eddie." Eddie proclaimed but no one was paying attention.

JULIA, was looking my way when she leaned over and whispered into Kristy's ear, "He's hot!"

"Hi ladies. Nice to meet you. Chuck's had a bit too much to drink," I said.

"Hiiiii!!!" Kristy replied.

"I think we should share a table with these nice girls and their friends," Rick suggested.

"Sounds like a great plan," Chuck agreed.

"Isn't Britt..." Ah, fuck it. What was the point? I guess we were staying.

A waitress came by and took our order. Chuck gave her his credit card and told her we wanted to run a tab. Chuck knows he can trust us. Rick was getting pretty lit. He was ordering shots for the girls and anyone else that walked by.

"So, what do you do?" Kristy asked me in a sort of nosey way.

"I'm a network engineer." That's my pat answer when I don't want to get into it with someone. She's not going to ask me any more questions about my job because she knows it will be technical and boring.

The Cowboys drove the ball right down the field in their first possession and scored a touchdown to end the kicking competition. They were up ten to nothing. The game was starting to feel like the beginning stages of the flu.

Kristy and Julia had some other friends but no one I was interested in. Eddie was still texting. He was surrounded by real women but was more interested in the virtual variety.

Chuck likes to have fun but Britt had nothing to worry about. He likes to be the one that connects others. If he were attempting to meet these women on his own, it would be a different story. Then he would be stammering and sweaty.

Rick ordered some more shots. I really don't want to down shots on a Sunday afternoon but felt compelled to do so. Chuck was all for it.

The shot guy is sort of passive aggressive. He portrays himself as the life of the party but he's really putting everyone in a bad spot. I mean, there's no turning back once you start with shots. "Hey let's all do shots!" is only a few steps away from "Let's all quit our jobs!" or "Fuck the police!"

"Come on man. Lighten up. We're having a good time. Fuck the game! We're surrounded by Philadelphia's finest," Chuck slurred in my direction.

A shot of Jameson was on the table in front of me. Fuck it.

Jameson goes down like liquid staples. I've never understood shots. Drinking is sort of like riding a bucking bronco; you're trying to stay on for as long as possible. Drinking shots is the equivalent of jabbing a nail in the before mentioned bronco's ass. I've never awakened the day after drinking shots and proclaimed, "Sure glad I drank shots last night."

Rick slammed his shot and then yelled "Woohoo!" for no apparent reason.

Kristy was still making eyes at me. I wasn't interested. Sometimes I wished I could be more like Eddie.

"Eddie, you should meet Kristy. Kristy, Eddie was one of the top sales reps at the Phone Company!" I made a pathetic attempt to pass Kristy off to Eddie. Eddie looked up from his phone and flashed a wide smile. Kristy was less than pleased.

The Cowboys scored again. Watching the Cowboys score was like watching your sister get raped. Our worst fear is to lose to the

Cowboys at home. The game seemed like it was going to end badly and add to the regret we'd feel from overindulging.

Since the game was so depressing, people were paying less attention to it and focused more on becoming as numb as possible. Rick ordered another round of shots.

There were a few pitchers of beer on our table. People that weren't even "with" our group were filling their glasses with our beer. The shot totals were getting bigger. At one point the waitress came over with an entire tray filled with shot glasses.

I know I was going to have to pay for everything. I have plenty so it's no big deal, but I wasn't happy about the way it was all going down. Rick was ordering food, drinks and shots for anyone within earshot of our table. He was spending my money. Chuck was just having a good time. Chuck deserved to have a good time with all that he'd been through. Eddie was half in and half out.

Late in the third quarter the Eagles finally scored. They kicked a field goal. The bar patrons gave a sarcastic cheer. As the game wound down, I noticed people leaving our party and heading out of the bar. Really, only Chuck, Rick and Eddie knew I had money. Everyone else was just taking advantage of the situation.

"You're the man!" Rick said to me.

If I acknowledged that I indeed was the man, would I be signing off on the mounting bar bill?

Rick was the weak link in our circle of friends. He was the most fearful and had the least going for him. There was nothing that Rick did exceedingly well. If he had been born twenty years earlier, it wouldn't have been a problem. He would have made a good living at the phone company and been able to retire comfortably. Now, who knew? We liked him because he seemed to like us. It would have been too much trouble to send him away but he wasn't really contributing. Lately, we had to deal with his mood swings and anxiety. I wish I had got to know Rick under a different set of circumstances. We had just become friends before Eddie and I landed the movie theater deal. That seemed to taint our friendship but Rick wouldn't let go. Eddie and I were like a sore in Rick's mouth that he couldn't stop touching with his tongue.

The fourth began the same way that the third did, with the Cowboys driving right down the field and the Eagles' defense powerless to stop them. Watching the Cowboys' players celebrate in our end zone made me consider giving up watching football altogether. There's no downside to watching a great movie but being an Eagles' fan could be like dating a super hot girl who periodically cheats on you. When a game goes like this one, you want to break up with your team. But then they'd win a game in spectacular fashion and it would be like the hot girlfriend giving you head while one of her friends watched.

The game ended with three straight Cowboy interceptions. The Eagles' production that day: Nine punts, three interceptions and one for two on field goal attempts. There couldn't have been a worse scenario. Lost at home? Check. Lost to the Cowboys? Check. No offense? Check. A defense as limp as an eighty year old man's penis? Check. Rick spending your money like it was made out of rotten banana peels? Check.

When the game finally ended, people cleared from our table like cockroaches in a suddenly illuminated kitchen. In less than ten seconds it was just Chuck, me, Eddie and Rick. The waitress came over, handed Chuck the tab and asked him if he would like to put everything on his card.

From the look on Chuck's face I knew it was substantial. Before I could offer to pay. Chuck looked at Rick and said, "We owe a hundred and fifty plus a tip, EACH." As you can tell, he emphasized the word, "each."

Chuck was ready to pay his share. It was his goal to treat me like everyone else - no better or worse.

"Fuck that. Let him pay," Rick exclaimed, looking in my direction.

Chuck's face got red. Eddie wasn't paying attention.

"You were the one ordering everybody shots, Rick," Chuck fired back.

Before I could step in and prevent what was about to happen, Rick went off. "I'm so fucking sick of you acting like Declan's just a regular guy. He has millions," he said and elongated the word "millions" to about three times its length.

"Declan could buy this bar right now. He could buy this whole block. He has more money than you and I will ever see in our lifetime."

"It doesn't mean we should spend it for him," Chuck shot back.

"Guys, give me the bill. I'll pay it."

"No fucking way. Rick's the asshole that invited people over and ordered all the shots."

"Fuck you, Chuck!" Rick replied. "Why don't you crawl further up Declan's ass?"

Eddie finally reappeared from his virtual world. "What's goin on?" he slurred.

"Fucking Rick is trying to saddle Declan with the bill," Chuck explained.

"Seriously, give me the bill. Who needs this shit?"

Chuck continued to clutch the objectionable bill with a fist that was now as red as his face.

"I didn't even want you to come today, Rick. I thought Eddie got on my nerves but you take the cake."

Eddie seemed pleased that he was no longer Chuck's most disliked friend.

"Why do you care so much Chuck? It's not your money. Do you know what six hundred is to Declan?

Rick was right. Knowing Chuck's approximate net worth and completing the math in my head, six hundred to me would be equivalent to twenty cents to Chuck.

"Declan you're such an asshole. You got Chuck here fooled. He thinks you're just one of us. You got so much money and you walk around like a nobody. Fuck, you still drive an Element!"

Hey, I liked my car. Plenty of space...sit up high...

Rick continued with his spew of hatred, "Why don't you help one of us out? You wouldn't even notice the difference. Why can't you be like some black basketball player?"

I was ready to pay. I didn't start the argument, Chuck and Rick did. Now Rick was coming after me.

"Is that what you want, Rick? A handout? I just wanted us all to remain friends. That's why I try to downplay the money."

"Yeah, you put on quite a show. Look at the jeans you're wearing. Where did you get them, Costco?"

Actually yes. What was wrong with Costco?

"You had too much to drink, the both of you. You're going to regret all this tomorrow."

"Fuck that! I'm not even drunk," Rick proclaimed.

Why do drunk people always defend their sobriety?

"I can't stand it anymore. I've never known anyone who was less fun than you. You were more fun when you didn't have money, and you weren't fun then. You just sit back and let us all amuse you. Instead of a car collection, you have us."

That was it. Rick struck a nerve. I always thought I was letting other people talk. Who cared what I had to say?

"Rick, you want some money? How much will it take to make you go away? A million? How about two?"

Everyone got silent and all eyes were on Rick.

Rick didn't want to say no.

"I'll make you a deal. I'll write you a check for two million, right here. But you have to disappear. I don't ever want to see or hear from you again."

Rick remained silent. He was too chicken shit to audibly agree or turn down my offer.

I pulled out my wallet. Still silence. Chuck and Eddie were in shock. I could tell Rick was going to accept the check. It was like we were playing a hand of poker and I was about to go all in and he was sitting on a royal flush. All he had to do was keep his mouth shut and control his emotions.

I pulled out an old, frayed check that I kept in my wallet in case of an emergency and used the pen that the waitress left behind to write out the check. Eddie and Chuck's eyes were more wide open than DeSean Jackson had ever been. Still nothing from Rick.

At this point the six hundred dollar check was about to become a two million, six hundred dollar check, or roughly six hundred and seventy dollars in Chuck's eyes.

I finished writing out the check and extended my arm in Rick's direction.

No one else in the bar knew what was going on. It was just the four of us and silence. Rick had a different future staring straight at him.

My arm remained extended for close to two minutes and then Rick reached out, took the check and left the bar in seconds. From the look on Chuck and Eddie's faces you'd think that they had just witnessed the resurrection.

I looked at those two and said, "What about you two?" I didn't have to go into any more detail.

Both Chuck and Eddie quickly turned me down. I think we all could have passed a breathalyzer that we would have failed miserably only five minutes prior.

The next day I stopped payment on the check. Fuck Rick.

CHAPTER 12

◄○►

CHUCK INVITED ME OVER FOR DINNER. I brought a bottle of Biondi Santi Brunello de Montalcino Riserva 2001, I had no idea if that was a good bottle of wine or not. I just bought the most expensive bottle of wine I could find at one of Pennsylvania's beautiful and convenient wine and spirits stores.

I loved Britt for Chuck. She was the sweetest, most loving girl a guy could ever want. She takes care of Chuck and all his baggage better than Chuck's mom would have. Chuck had been through the ringer, relationship wise. Not that a lot of it wasn't his fault. He was stubborn and inflexible. Britt was perfect for him because she was the opposite. There was the weight issue but Britt was trying. Funny thing about Chuck was, the weight thing had affected prior relationships but every girl he dated was a little bigger than the girl before. When I asked him about that one time, he replied, "I know. Crazy, right? I guess subconsciously, I must like it."

Chuck found Britt on a BBW dating site. He thought he might find a big chested woman on there. He was on the site for less than a month. Talk about the sky opening. Those two just clicked and have been together ever since.

Britt was part Spic (her words) and had a beautiful face with big, brown eyes and long dark hair. She used to make fun of Chuck's eyes because they were smaller. She called them his "tinesters". Then Chuck retaliated by referring to her eyes as "saucers". You can see where this is going. You know how some people can get a little weird if they spend too much time alone? Chuck and Britt might be the couple equivalent.

"Hey look, it's Mr. Big Shot, Britt. He showed up on time for once," Chuck said with a big smile.

"I took the train." Which was a running joke based on the location of Chuck's residence in relationship to the railroad tracks.

"Hi, Declan," Britt sang as much as she spoke the words as she hugged and kissed my cheek.

"Hello sweetheart," I replied. I didn't even call some of my former girlfriends 'sweetheart.'

Chuck's dog Bunk came over and paid his respects and then went back to sleep on the living room rug.

"He doesn't bark when you come to the door. He must know your scent. Anyone else, he scares the shit out of," Chuck informed me.

After Bunk, Chuck's cats took a turn. It was like an animal procession line. Robin, Chuck's girl cat, probably loved Chuck more than Britt did. Chuck liked calling Robin "sweetheart" and "honey" to get under Britt's skin. Britt liked calling Robin a "whore." When Robin came in from the outdoors, Britt would look down at her and ask, "Where have you been?" the same way a mother would question her daughter if she arrived home after curfew. Howard, the brother, didn't have a care. He had the loudest purr I've ever heard. He would lay out on the floor with his head in his food dish and eat. You could hear him purring from across the room.

"Wow, this is some bottle of wine," Britt exclaimed when I handed her the bottle.

She knew what she was talking about because she was gourmet and had been working in the hospitality business for the last ten years.

"Declan, I'm getting tired of you showing up alone. Don't tell me you can't find someone," Britt paused. "Chuck did."

Britt had this way of delivering a shot that never made it objectionable. She made her eyes big and then hit you with a glorious smile.

"He's got women throwing themselves at him. He has to be careful. They might be after the wrong thing," Chuck said.

"You sure don't have that worry," Britt fired back with her eyebrows raised.

Chuck loved Britt's sense of humor.

"Shouldn't you be in the kitchen preparing our dinner?" Chuck replied, emphasizing the word "our".

"Want a beer?" Chuck asked me.

"Sure."

"Good thing I still have some of the beer you brought here on Sunday."

"Have you heard from Rick?" I asked.

"No. What about you?"

"No, but that was the deal we struck."

"But you didn't hold up your end of the bargain. He has every right to be seen or heard by you."

"Good one," I replied. "Would you have given him the money?"

"I wouldn't have made the offer in the first place. That was some crazy shit, from what I can remember."

"It was one ugly scene. I appreciate your support, by the way. But next time, just let me pay."

"It was the principal."

"I know but we only have two friends left and you're not nuts about one of them."

Britt entered the room with a spoon in one hand and an oven mitt on the other.

"Chuck told me what happened. What do I have to do to get one of those checks?" Britt asked with a curious look and then flashed the smile.

Chuck made this get back in the kitchen signal with this hand. His palm was pointed towards the floor and his fingers were spread apart. He flicked his wrist a couple of times to send Britt on her way.

"I hate you," Britt sang as she walked back to the kitchen.

Chuck and I sat in the living room, sipping beer and waiting for Britt to call us to dinner.

"I was walking Bunk in the park yesterday and some guy was about to pass us on his bike and he chimed a bell to let me know. I fucking told him he could stick his bell up his ass."

"Did he stop?"

"No, just kept riding."

"You're supposed to say, 'on your left' or 'on your right.' I don't say anything."

"Last thing I would do is ring a fucking bell."

"How's business?"

"It's been picking up. I would be great if I could get everyone to pay on time."

"You're really getting good."

"Thanks. Just glad that I'm not working for the phone company anymore. I heard it's a real bitchfest over there."

It was the opposite of growing pains; I guess you would call them shrinking pains. There was a time when a company would be happy to pay the phone company a thousand dollars per month for a single T1. Now, a broadband connection providing fifty times the speed could be purchased for a little more than a tenth of the price. But it's not like one day all the sales people are getting fat and happy and the next they're gone. It's long, grueling process that's no fun for anyone.

"You guys," Britt called us from the kitchen. "It's ready!"

"You really got the setup and you don't even know it," I told Chuck.

"You know I love her."

We all sat down at the table in Chuck and Britt's dining area, just off the kitchen. If it was just Chuck, we'd be eating on the couch. Britt somehow made the place look quaint. Britt was a master wrapper; she would wrap gifts so nice that you wouldn't want to open them. She did the same sort of thing with Chuck's place. I was there before she arrived and I would describe Chuck's taste to be somewhere between shabby shit and stench.

Bunk came in and sniffed the table a few times. He was so tall; he could rest his chin on the top of the table. Chuck trained him though. Old Bunk would never try to grab and run. Chuck told me that Bunk always eats his food when they're eating. He thinks it's because Bunk's sense of smell is so strong. Bunk eats his food while smelling the aroma of Chuck and Britt's food. Bunk's done it so many times that Chuck's convinced. Chuck observes Bunk closely. He's the Jane Goodall of Bunk.

"This sure is some fancy wine. Don't spill it Chuck," Britt said to Chuck while he was opening the bottle. "I'm so excited!"

Chuck was struggling with the bottle opener. He couldn't get the corkscrew to line up in the center of the cork. He made three attempts and then looked up at the ceiling to reboot himself.

"Idiot!" Britt let out.

Chuck's fourth attempt was a charm.

"It'll probably taste the same as every other bottle of wine we've ever drank," Chuck stated.

"You are some pill," Britt said to Chuck.

"Cheers!" Britt said as she raised her glass.

We all took a drink and it was good. Not four hundred dollars a bottle good but close. Eddie would have said it best. "For four hundred bucks I'd expect to be blown while I was drinking it."

"How's the steak?" Britt asked. Food was very important to Britt.

"Great! So tender," I replied.

"We switched from gas to charcoal," Chuck proclaimed.

"We had enough gas with Chuck and Bunk in the house," Britt fired and then flashed the smile.

"Charcoal's supposed to taste better. Gas might be easier but that's until you run out of propane. Then you got to go to a gas station and hope the attendant isn't too busy to get you a new tank. Charcoal is messier but at least you can purchase charcoal almost anywhere." Chuck thought about every little detail.

"Honey, why don't you pull out a whiteboard and diagram the differences between gas and charcoal? I don't think you've gone into enough detail." Britt exclaimed.

"What time did you leave this morning?" Chuck asked Britt.

"Don't ask. Very early. You were sound asleep."

"You can wake me up. I don't mind. I'd make you coffee if there were any to-go cups left in the house. You never bring them back home. We need some come-back cups."

"Good one," Britt commented. They didn't always laugh at each other's jokes and puns but "good one" was as good as a laugh to Chuck and Britt.

"There was an NRA meeting at the hotel today," Britt informed us. "There were protesters outside, news cameras… I told Marie not to book the meeting, but she never listens to me."

Marie was Britt's general manager.

"If there was a right to drive amendment, there would be no fuel efficiency regulations or safety standards; you wouldn't have to get your vehicle inspected; one hundred year olds would still have their licenses…" Chuck summarized.

"Where did you walk Bunk, sweetheart?" Britt asked, cutting Chuck off before he built up a full head of steam.

"I walked him down past Henkel's, under the train tracks, up Sumac, through the park, past the ugly elementary school, past Custard Creamery and Rita's, past the bowling alley…"

"Okay," Britt tried to interrupt.

"Through the ugly apartments…" Chuck continued.

"Okay."

"Down the asthma steps…"

"Sweetheart! Don't forget that Declan's here. He's the only friend of yours I like," She said then smiled at me. "Did you hit your head on your walk?" Britt asked as she examined Chuck's head with a concerned look on her face.

"Bunk dumped right in front a family sitting out on their porch."

"Oh, God! Did you have a bag?" Britt asked.

"I always have a bag. Some of them just have holes in them," Chuck replied.

Chuck had to use grocery store plastic bags because Bunk's bowel movements were so large.

"This one wasn't one of his soliders." Chuck and Britt liked to make up words.

Britt gagged. She made this perfect gag sound whenever she was disgusted by Chuck or Bunk.

"What did you do?" Britt asked Chuck apprehensively.

"I just grabbed what I could (more Britt gagging) and walked away as fast as possible. Then three houses down, he did a doubler." More Britt and Chuck speak. "I didn't have a second bag, so I acted like it was just gas and kept walking. I better avoid that street for a while."

"I told Chuck we were out of butter," Britt started. "He took Bunk and walked down Cresson to the market underneath the rail line, Palm something. Anyway, he got the butter and he walked back on Main Street. It was a nice day, so a bunch of people were outside dining and drinking. Chuck ran into a client, talked to that guy. He bumped into one of our old neighbors, talked to her. Saw a couple he knew from networking, sitting down eating dinner and talked to them. He came home carrying this plastic bag with the butter in it. He listed everyone he saw and spoke to. I asked him, what they thought he had in the bag. Chuck turned even more white. I think he became pale." Big finish. Big smile.

Chuck was laughing, red faced. All I could think of was Chuck prancing down Main with the loaded bag in his hand, waving it around, talking to everyone.

Just then a train passed. It startled me but Chuck and Britt hardly seemed to notice.

"You guys don't even notice the trains anymore, do you?"

"Did one just pass?" Britt asked and then flashed a smile.

Britt reached over and put her hand gently on Chuck's. "Sweetheart," Britt cooed "Can we please find a normal place to live?"

"What's wrong with this place?"

"Why do I love you?" Britt asked, not expecting an answer.

"What made you pick this place?" I asked Chuck.

"I liked the location. When the stairs existed, I could walk to CVS in two minutes."

"Ah, the finer things," Britt said.

Chuck was pissed that the city removed a set of stairs that lead from the back of his house down to Main Street.

"There are stairs all over this town and they decide to remove the ones right behind my house!"

"Hopefully, the next thing the city removes will be this house." Britt said.

"Let them try," Chuck challenged.

"You're going to take the city on now?" Britt asked.

"I'll take on the whole state, if I have to," Chuck boasted.

"I know you would sweetheart," Britt responded and then looked my way and rolled her eyes.

"Did Chuck tell you we went to see The Book of Mormon?" Britt asked.

"No. How was it?"

"It was okay," Chuck started. "Have you ever seen a really famous comedian perform? You know how the crowd busts out laughing at everything he says? It was like that. It was funny but not as funny as the crowd was reacting."

"It was funny," Britt proclaimed.

"And those South Park guys aren't accomplished songwriters," Chuck continued, ignoring Britt's comment. "They used too many words. You could hardly understand what they were singing half the time."

"Only you…" I replied.

"I had to sit by myself because Britt was with her mom in the herniated disc section. I was in between two couples that were laughing hysterically. The play makes fun of a major religion, discusses baby rape, details dysentery; in one scene Jeffrey Dahmer is butt fucking somebody's dad and Hitler is receiving fellatio and everyone in the theater's laughing so hard they can barely breathe. This one old couple made it through three quarters of the play and then left after the big dick scene.

"But listen to this. I went up the concession stand. Of course they don't sell popcorn. I ordered a bag of peanuts and a large soda that was smaller than a venti at Starbucks. It was thirteen dollars! I went to hand the lady my card and she tells me they have a fifteen dollar minimum. She wanted to charge me two more dollars if I used my card. Forget that! Think about it. The peanuts and soda couldn't cost them more than a dollar. They just passed up a thirteen hundred percent profit because they didn't want to pay a percentage to a credit card company."

That was Chuck's life. It was all about the little things. Little things upset him and little things made him happy. Hugging Bunk made the rest of the world disappear but a bad experience at the concession stand would be the only thing he'd remember from a fun night out.

"Hey, that whole thing with Rick got me thinking," I started abruptly.

Britt and Chuck could tell I was starting something serious.

"I love you guys. I mean, you've been there for me, without fail. You've never asked me for anything, ever. You helped me feel normal.

"I basically won the lottery. I was at the right place at the right time, with the right skill set. I mean, when we all started at the phone company, we were pretty much equals. No disrespect."

"None taken," Chuck replied.

"That whole thing with the MovieDate just fell in my lap. It was like the sky opened up and there it was.

"The greatest thing about having all the money is I'll never have to worry about it again. I gave Rick the check to get rid of him. Unlike you guys, Rick has always been jealous.

"I have more than I need. I want to give you something and I don't want you to say no. Please, don't say no. Just take it. I love you guys so much and I want you to be relieved of any of your worries."

I laid out a check on the table. Britt's eyes were watering. My eyes were watering.

"Is this because of that crap with Rick?" Chuck asked.

"I've been thinking about this for some time. The thing with Rick just brought it to the forefront. It helped me identify who my true friends are."

The check sat unchecked for the duration of dinner. Chuck and Britt had no idea how much it was for. I gave the same amount to Eddie.

The next day I'd be leaving town.

CHAPTER 13

◄○►

I DECIDED IT WOULD BE A GOOD time to leave Philadelphia. Usually, I hung around the city until the first snowfall but after the experience with Rick, I thought it was better to take off now.

I like doing things my own way; that's probably why I am still single. Most people who wanted to get away would buy a plane ticket and fly to a vacation spot. Not me. I liked to pretend; make believe that I was in a movie or a novel.

If you grew up in Philadelphia, you probably know Joey Coyle's story. He was the everyday schmo who found a big bag of money that fell out of an armored car. Joey did just about everything wrong afterwards and almost went to jail. Eddie and I used to debate what we would have done differently. Eddie said he would have stowed the money in his attic and do his best to forget about it. Then years later, he would retire somewhere tropical and pay for everything in cash. I said that I would have figured out a way to spread the money around in one of the depressed parts of Philadelphia.

"Why would you do something stupid like that?" Eddie asked me.

139

"I don't know. I wouldn't feel comfortable keeping the money. I didn't want to say that I'd just give it back," I replied.

"It's not like they'd use the money for anything decent. The area Cadillac and Lincoln dealers would see a spike in sales, but that would be about it."

"That wasn't too racist."

"The safest thing to do would be to give it to the older women in the community. They'd make sure it was put to good use."

"How do you give that much money away without drawing attention to yourself?"

"It would require a lot of work. You'd have to stake out the area and then put envelopes of money in the old ladies' mail slots."

"It's too easy for us because we're single. It would be more of a quandary if we were married and had kids. Would you tell your wife? Would she be willing to go along with you if you wanted to keep the money?"

"Good point. What if you were married and hated your wife? That money could be your ticket out."

"Only you, Eddie."

Stories about found money used to fascinate me. "Used to" is the key phrase because after I became rich, the fascination sort of dissipated. I wanted to recapture the feeling.

I decided to pretend that I was a wanted fugitive running from the law.

What did I do wrong?

Nothing violent, that's for sure.

What if I was an embezzler?

First step, I needed cash.

If you're a wanted fugitive you can't pay for anything with a credit card and anything larger than a twenty could draw suspicion. I headed to the bank and requested forty thousand dollars in twenty dollar bills.

The teller I spoke to asked me to take a seat in the customer lounge and wait for a bank manager to help me. Shortly after, one of the bank managers came over and asked me to follow him to his office.

I had dealt with that bank manager before.

"How are you today, Declan?"

"I'm doing fine. How are you?"

"Fine, fine.

"So you want to deduct forty thousand from your account. Is everything okay?"

"Oh sure. Why do you ask?

"Just making sure you're not under any duress, or something like that?"

"Oh no. You mean like a kidnap?"

"That sounds a little harsh, but that or maybe someone is extorting you… it's always good to ask just in case. Hope you weren't offended in any way?"

The bank manager was a younger fellow that dressed like he wore his father's hand me downs. He was friendly and wanted to be cool but that would be a difficult goal to achieve due to his general appearance. Glasses, a soft, puffy body, his dad's outdated wardrobe and a slightly orange complexion destined him to be what he had become, a bank manager.

"Oh no. Thanks. I appreciate your concern. No, all's good. Just headed to Vegas."

I wasn't headed to Vegas but thought it would be the easiest explanation.

He smiled and proclaimed, "Of what I'd do to be in your shoes.

"You know the old bank manager, her family was held at gunpoint. There were these two guys, one stayed with the family and the other followed her to the bank. She was supposed to give the one that was with her a hundred grand so they'd release her family."

"No, shit."

"Yes. She got the money but did it in a way to tip off the other bank employees. The police followed her and the guy back to her home and waited for the two hooligans to leave the house and then took 'em down.

"No one was hurt and the bank didn't lose any money. She received a nice accommodation. She had a pretty good sense of humor about the experience. If you called her home after the incident and reached her voicemail, the message said, *Sorry we're all tied up and can't answer the phone right now…*" The bank manager thought that was quite comical and laughed like he just heard the message for the first time. "So you can't be too sure.

"Plus, we just had that very large stop payment situation."

"Oh yeah, sorry about that."

"No problem. That's what we're here for. You know, we have financial managers on staff. I could schedule you an appointment to meet with one of them?"

"No, I'm fine, but just a heads up, there's going to be a couple more. Not stop payments but real checks."

"We're going to have to have you followed."

"Really?"

"No, just kidding," he said laughing. "But seriously, you're okay?" he asked with a concerned look on his face.

"Yes. Yes. You know, if you want to drive home with me…"

"I wouldn't mind going to Vegas with you, I can tell you that. I'd love to get the heck out of this place. The new general manager is a real ball buster, if you catch my drift?" The manager said under his breath.

The manager picked up his desk phone and instructed the person on the other end to deliver the money to his office.

"Just a few more moments and I'll get you out of here. Do you want it in a bag?"

"No. I brought a duffel bag," I replied as I handed it to him.

I wondered how I would have received the money if I didn't bring the duffel. I don't think it would be a good idea to walk out of a bank with a couple of stuffed bank bags. Even a briefcase might be an issue. You know, walking out of a bank with any container other than a cardboard box full of your personal belongings is probably a bit risky. Although, I don't think there are people that sit outside banks waiting for bag holders. That wouldn't be a good use of time, would it?

I collected the money and scurried to my car before any bank stalkers could get at me.

Next stop, a used car lot. I wanted it to be one of those single owner deals. Some ambitious, can't work for anybody type of sales guy who figured out how to open his own lot. My house is close to Ridge Avenue, which cuts through Roxborough. If you drive down Ridge, it's a never-ending freak show; one unusual storefront after another and each person you see is stranger than the last.

On Ridge, I found Auto Maxx Motors. It was perfect. There was a small sales building, surrounded by random cars and streamers dangling from the telephone lines strung overhead (wait, how is that okay?) There were sales banners everywhere and almost as many American flags, letting everyone know that Auto Maxx was American owned and operated.

I didn't want to drive on the lot so I parked my car at a nearby grocery store and walked over. I was greeted by Gigi Kiza, a man of East Indian descent, who delivered a great big smile and won me over instantly. My only concern was whether or not Gigi would have a car that appealed to me.

"Hello, hello!" Gigi exclaimed. "It's always a good sign when a potential customer walks on the lot," Gigi said with a hearty laugh.

"Yes, I guess so. But you're still going to have to earn my business."

"We wouldn't want it any other way."

Gigi had a completely round head. It helped that he was mostly bald. He wasn't handsome but looked like he took a good photo.

"Good. Here's what I am looking for…"

I told him I needed an older, eight-cylinder, American car. I wanted it to go fast and handle poorly. It would be a plus if there was a strong possibility that it would break down. Breakdowns would lead to interactions with small town mechanics that may or may not attempt to rip me off.

"I have the perfect car!"

He took me outside and around back and there it was, a 1984 Pontiac Firebird. It was the perfect car. It had no flashy extras that could draw attention, like two toned paint or a flaming phoenix painted on the hood. It also had stained plush seating and some aftermarket cup holders.

The car was listed for ten thousand. It was in pretty decent shape and the mileage was reasonable.

"Isn't that a bit much for an old car?" I asked.

"For this car?" Gigi asked as he lowered his glasses and looked me in the eye. "This is a collector's item. They're in very high demand."

"I don't think I would pay you more than eight for it."

"You're obviously not a collector. Maybe we should look for something newer, more practical?"

Here I was a multimillionaire squabbling over a couple thousand dollars. Wait, that's what he wanted me to think.

"I'll give you nine."

"Ninety-five."

"Fine."

Some negotiator I was. But good thing I wasn't the one that sold MovieDate.

I followed Gigi into his office. I pulled out five stacks of twenties from my duffle, took twenty-five off the top of one stack, and handed the money over to Gigi. He looked impressed.

"You know, we have some much nicer cars. It's not too late, if you'd like to take a look?"

"No. We're good."

Gigi wasn't worried about insurance. We took care of the tags and registration and I was out of there.

"Just remember me. Anything you need. Car, boat, small plane..." Gigi proclaimed as I was pulling away.

Unfortunately, I had to interrupt my fantasy and call my insurance agent and have her add the car to my policy. Maybe I'm silly but I'm not stupid.

The car moved like a 35 year old, NFL running back that took one too many hits. The seats felt compressed. I thought about how they were the original seat covers and that I was sitting on 30 years of farts and who knows what. Would a fugitive stop to buy new seat covers?

I had to get out of Pennsylvania. Any cool movie driving sequence happened on open roads. Pennsylvania roads are too claustrophobic, especially the turnpike. The road travels through thick forest and wooded hills. Only in few occasions is there is any sort of scenery.

People don't understand how big Pennsylvania is. It takes six hours to transverse the state. Fortunately, the flaming bird was running smoothly. Its radio was delivering something less than entertainment though.

Road trips seem so appealing in movies because they're not shown in real time. Maybe I should have flown down south and then purchased a car? Couldn't risk the airport security. What was my goal? Obviously, I needed to head somewhere far away that was less metropolitan. North or south? South obviously; winter was coming.

I hadn't planned my escape route. I couldn't use my phone. Wait, what was I doing with a cell phone when I was a wanted fugitive? I had to toss it. Really? In the movies, they take the battery out and break the phone. Once the battery is out, I would assume the phone is untrackable. I decided to start with battery and see how that went. Who needed a phone anyway? Time began to slow.

Would a fugitive purchase a GPS?

A sign on the turnpike informed me that there was a rest stop in three miles.

Turnpike rest stops are filled with every dope that thought a long, road trip made sense. They're one of the few places on earth where everyone present wishes they were somewhere else.

I used the restroom and then purchased an ice coffee, a bottle of water, a bag of almonds, a GPS and some stylish seat covers.

I entered my semi alma mater, The University of Arizona into the GPS. I probably could have made it there without its help but I liked knowing where I was and didn't want to get lost when I left a freeway.

I was driving; I had GPS to guide me, but wasn't sure I would cooperate.

CHAPTER 14

I DECIDED TO BLITZ THROUGH PENNSYLVANIA, WEST
Virginia and Ohio. I wanted to drive ninety but couldn't afford
to get pulled over. Declan could afford it, but I wasn't Declan,
remember. I needed an assumed name. How about Eddie Bezzler?

Who the heck was Eddie Bezzler?

Just a regular guy. He was living two lives: one with his wife and
kids and a second, secret life. Eddie's secret life was being funded,
unknowingly, by his boss. He managed a car wash and was pocketing
most of the cash customers' money.

Why did he do it?

He fell in love with a younger woman and the only way he felt
he could hold onto her was by showering her with gifts. He couldn't
use his own money because his wife would have found out.

Well, she was going to find out anyway but Eddie's way delayed
the process. For weeks, he lived on the edge. There wasn't a single
moment when he wasn't thinking of the girl or about the possibility
of getting caught. Unlike other embezzlers, he had no delusions of

ever repaying his boss. He decided there was only one course; it was one way and dead-ended at the edge of a cliff.

It had been five months and Eddie had pocketed close to ten thousand dollars. Not a huge amount but one he couldn't repay. Eddie's boss, the owner, trusted him. He'd been working at the car wash for ten years and been a model employee for nine years and seven months. Then she walked in.

Before I describe the woman, I need to explain Eddie.

Eddie was breast obsessed. Not with just any pair of breasts - they had to be big - in fact - the bigger the better. From the moment he first saw a photo of a large breasted woman in a Playboy magazine when he was thirteen that was it. That's how he knew gay guys didn't choose to be gay. He knew because he didn't make a choice to like large breasts, he just liked them.

Not long after he saw the photo of the woman in Playboy, one of his schoolmates blossomed. Kathy Long blossomed in middle school. She played field hockey and Eddie had trouble walking after witnessing her sprint across the playing field.

Then there was Ms. Tietsworth, who lived up to her name. She was Eddie's art teacher. Ms. Tietsworth might have caught Eddie massaging a ball of clay a little too aggressively while staring at her. Eddie was in a bit of a trance when it happened, so he's not a hundred percent sure.

If Eddie knew where a big-breasted girl lived and happened to be walking past her house, just thinking about the girl would arouse him. When Eddie sold Christmas wreaths for the boy scouts, he made a point to visit the well-endowed girls' houses. He created fantasies and possible scenarios in his head. Sadly, none of them came true.

As Eddie grew older, so did his desire. Problem was, Eddie was a skinny kid with acne. No girls were interested in Eddie, especially the ones he wanted. Eddie figured every male shared his obsession. Eddie didn't go after what he wanted because he figured that those girls could do better than him. He lacked confidence. When he tried to talk to a big-breasted girl he would mumble and shake.

Eddie struggled through high school and started to blossom in college. It didn't matter though because he couldn't keep his cool around women with large breasts. There were five women that Eddie figured he could have slept with and realized his dream, but for one reason or another it didn't happen. If Eddie started to think about the different women and each set of circumstances, it would cause him physical pain.

The first girl wanted to sleep with Eddie. He met her at a frat party and she invited him back to her dorm room. She was a discus thrower on Eddie's track team. She had enormous breasts, much bigger than any he'd seen in a magazine. Eddie was drunk and stupid. When they arrived at the girl's room her roommate was present. When the girl went off to find them another place to romp, he made a pass at the roommate, who didn't have big breasts and wasn't even attractive. When the large breasted girl returned, her roommate ratted on Eddie. Eddie was shown the door.

Then there was the girl in Eddie's Poli Sci class. Poli Sci was one of the few subjects Eddie excelled in. Eddie and this girl were somewhere in between acquaintances and friends. Eddie remembered locking eyes with her in a stairwell and how she smiled at him. It wasn't just any smile; she liked him. She asked Eddie to tutor her. She had incredible breasts. When Eddie walked into her dorm room, he saw one of her bras slung over a chair. It was the kind with six fasteners on the back and wire running below the cup. Eddie stuck to Political Science and walked home frustrated. The girl never invited him back.

The third girl, Eddie saw her on one of his first training runs with his college cross-country team. She was a tiny girl with huge boobs. Eddie spotted them fifty yards away. A year later, she was dating a guy that lived on Eddie's floor. He was blond, like Eddie, but not as handsome, at least in Eddie's mind. One day Eddie noticed she cut her hair and threw her a compliment when they passed on the stairs (always the stairs). She flashed a big smile and said thank you. Another time, when Eddie was making his rounds as a campus security guard, she answered the door of her sorority house in a nighty. Unfortunately, Eddie was making the rounds with a fellow security officer who couldn't stop giggling. If he had a gun he might have shot his giggling cohort. Instead, he kept his eyes up, obtained the girl's signature, thanked her and said good night. The last time, he saw her behind the library. Again she flashed a bright smile. It was the sort of smile from a woman that you might take for granted when you're a young man but would kill for after you turned forty. All he had to do was say "hi" and introduce himself. He didn't know much but something was telling him she was interested. He couldn't do it. He kept walking and never saw her again.

The fourth girl, Eddie went to high school with. She liked Eddie when no other girl gave him the time of day. She had enormous breasts, but he didn't really know it at the time because she hid them under bulky sweaters that made her look fat. Any girl that expressed interest in him was going to receive some consideration, however. But Eddie made the mistake of asking the captain of his track team for advice. The captain probably preferred skinny girls and told Eddie she looked fat. Eddie decided not to pursue her and graduated high school a frustrated virgin.

After Eddie graduated college, he ran into the girl at a local shopping center. Each of her breasts was bigger than his head. At that point in his life, Eddie had more experience with women and was able to make a date with her. They went out for a beer and a movie. Eddie still remembered the top she wore (tight black sweater) and the movie (The Fan, a movie Eddie couldn't stand because it had an English director who knew nothing about baseball. One of the game scenes was filmed in dark, rainy weather. How would that ever happen?) At some point in the movie, the girl leaned over to Eddie and stuck her tongue in his ear. Not only was that the most erotic thing Eddie had ever experienced in his young life, all the blood in his body flowed to his lower half. They made out for the rest of the movie.

Eddie and the girl were still living with their parents, so they had no place to go that had sheets and a mattress. Eddie drove her to the Valley Forge National Park. He knew a parking lot where they might find some privacy. Eddie swears that he'd never seen anyone in that lot at night. Not that evening. Inexplicably, a group of hobbyist were flying radio controlled planes in the dark sky. Eddie felt cursed.

There were probably a hundred other places he could have taken her to but he chose that place, and he could sense that the girl wasn't as desperate as he was becoming, so he took her home. Her dad was still up and in the other room. Eddie's demented brain felt that a girl with such large breasts must have been uninhibited sexually. He wouldn't stop kissing her or fondling her breasts over her sweater. At the peak of his frustration, they decided to call it a night. She walked him to his car and they kissed one last time. She had had it with his groping. She asked him why he wouldn't stop feeling her breasts. He didn't have a good answer.

After that night, she wouldn't return Eddie's calls. Eddie found out later that she got her own apartment two weeks after their fateful date.

Eddie ended up marrying a woman with small breasts. She had a great body but didn't need to wear a bra. She had long legs and a great ass, that probably made leg and ass men nuts and unable to speak to her but they had no effect on Eddie.

Three months after their wedding and one month before his wife was expecting their first child, Eddie went alone to the apartment complex pool. There was a woman at the pool whose breasts were so large she had to buy two bikinis; one that fit her top and another her bottom. That's the Holy Grail for a breast lover.

Eddie and the girl were alone together at one end of the pool. They struck up a conversation. The conversation went from "Hi. How are you?" to "I have to buy two different bikinis because my breasts are so big" in minutes. All Eddie had to do was ask her if she wanted to get something to drink. He could have easily steered her to her apartment. "My roommate's family is visiting," would have worked. But his new wife was sitting seven months pregnant in their apartment and he knew, sometime in the future, they'd run into the girl together.

The fifth girl hurt the worst. He asked his wife to marry him because she was pregnant. He never got a chance to be young and single. But he wouldn't have been at that pool if he wasn't married; he'd probably be still living with his parents. God was a bastard.

Years later, Eddie was behind the cash register at the car wash, when she walked in. She was everything he desired in a woman: She had enormous, shapely breasts that created an amazing display of cleavage, long curly hair that framed her beautiful face, a thin waist and a lovely round ass.

Eddie made her laugh the first time she visited the register. He was determined to make her a returning customer, so he created a three visits and your fourth wash is free promotion on the spot.

He couldn't get her out of his mind. Every time she came to the register his heart raced and his mind sharpened. Every time he made her laugh.

"You're cute," she said and smiled.

His heart melted. She gave him a high that he'd never felt before. He wasn't going to let this woman be number six on his list.

"You are too," he replied.

And then, a miracle happened. She wrote her phone number down on a slip of paper and handed it to him.

"Call me."

It couldn't be. The woman that made every man's head turn gave Eddie her phone number. He forgot about his wife and kids. There was no way he was going to pass on this girl.

Still skinny Eddie, the car wash employee, was operating way over his head. For her to overlook his bony body and Target wardrobe, it was a miracle. It was so unlikely that Eddie felt that it was meant to be. It was God's will, and who was he to question God?

They planned a date. Eddie told his wife he joined a bowling league. He bought a bowling ball and bowling shoes; even had a league shirt made. Then he put a change of clothes in the trunk of his car. His wife seemed happy that he found some friends.

Their date was at a trendy Asian restaurant. The final bill was two hundred dollars. Eddie had to act like it was no problem. He might have hinted that he owned the car wash. The fact that he didn't try to follow her home made her like him more. Normally Eddie would have acted like a puppy dog but he was thinking so hard about how he was going to pull the whole thing off that he didn't act needy or desperate.

That first date, she kissed him goodnight and a rush traveled down his spine. They decided to spend a weekend together. That was going to be difficult. Eddie told his wife he was attending a religious retreat. He had to book the room and pay for everything but he didn't care because he was going to get to sleep with his angel.

When you're making forty thousand a year and have a wife and two kids, you can't afford romantic getaways. That's when Eddie started dipping into the company coffer.

That first night was magical. Eddie felt twenty years younger. He made love like a lion. His lips and tongue touched every perfect square inch of the girl's body. She might as well have been meth because he was hooked. He didn't care about anything but her afterwards.

He rented a small, furnished apartment so he could have her over. He lied and lied and lied.

His boss wasn't usually around the car wash that much. But that changed. All of a sudden he was there on a regular basis. He had meetings with various people. Eddie was never invited to any of the meetings and every time they were alone together, Eddie's boss didn't say much.

Eddie knew what he had to do. He cashed out his IRA. He just had to wait for the check to arrive and then deposit it and wait for the money to be available. He checked his account three times a day. The day the funds were accessible, he made a withdrawal and split.

He told the girl he was considering expanding into Tucson. He was hoping that maybe he'd be able to establish himself there and she might follow. She wasn't going to want him if he was arrested. Of course it would be difficult to explain his name change and altered appearance.

CHAPTER 15

◄○►

EDDIE BEZZLER WAS ACTUALLY BASED ON my friend
Eddie. In college, we carried on long conversations during our
runs, and just about everywhere else on campus. It's safe to say that
I exchanged more words with Eddie than any other person I've ever
known.

Eddie was the type of person that would tell you anything if
he liked and trusted you, which in my case was after about fifteen
minutes. I knew Eddie's entire life story. He had a tale for just about
every circumstance and situation. And he'd tell you the same story
two or more times if you let him.

Eddie had a sex addiction. Not an addiction where he wasn't
able to function. I mean he wasn't like a homeless junkie, cruising
the streets, searching for his next fix. Eddie was a hardworking and
productive person, but he thought about sex almost every waking
hour.

Eddie was indeed breast obsessed. He was also a virgin when he
graduated high school. But Eddie didn't expect to have sex in high
school. In fact, he didn't think anyone was having sex in high school.

Eddie was a bit sheltered and naive. Eddie would tell you a story about something that occurred when he was a "kid" and it would turn out that it happened when he was sixteen or seventeen.

Eddie made it through his freshman year of college without getting laid. Mostly that was Eddie's fault because, due to our running schedule, we could only go out one night a week and when Eddie went out, he drank and Eddie drank for only one reason and that was to get bombed.

Eddie blamed his appearance for his lack of success with girls in high school and college. He was skinny, had bad skin and crooked teeth. He also lacked confidence. Women either found him unattractive due to his appearance or his lack of confidence. It was hard to tell which one because his appearance led to his lack of confidence.

Eddie had to be drunk to build up the nerve to talk to women but when he was drunk he was a bit of a mess. He tended to spit when he spoke. He became aware of that flaw after witnessing more than one woman wipe her face after he spoke to her. He tried looking in a different direction when he spoke or holding a cup in front of his mouth, but then he was hard to hear and understand. Eddie also had no patience for small talk and was totally bored by everyday conversation. So really, it would take an act of God to get Eddie laid in most party situations.

The first time Eddie had sex was outside a party, in the grass, next to a tree. He decided he had to end his drought anyway possible and approached literally the most unpleasant looking girl that attended our college. That was no easy feat because our school was famous for its physical educational program. There were girls that attended our college that were bigger and stronger than some of our football players. One parents' day, a smart ass hung a sheet on the outside of one of the dorms that read, "U College, where men are men, women are men and sheep run scared." Eddie started talking to the phys ed major. She mentioned that she had just bought a new car. He asked her to show it to him. They went outside together. He asked her if she'd ever been kissed next to her new car and two minutes later they were at it.

Eddie had to ask the girl to insert his penis because he'd never done it before or witnessed it being done in pornography. He thought the penis went straight down towards the buttocks, not up towards the stomach.

Less than fifteen minutes later, Eddie was propositioned by the big chested discus thrower.

Now, this is one of Eddie's great what ifs. What if Eddie had been patient and ended up with the discobolus as his first love? Maybe he would have had an entirely different college experience. Perhaps, they would have fallen in love and ended up getting married. What if he hadn't propositioned the roommate and an un-showered Eddie engaged in sexual activity with the discus thrower? Maybe she would have been totally disgusted and still thrown him out?

For the next two years there would be two constants in Eddie's sexual activity: He would be drunk and the girl would be unsatisfied.

Apparently, Eddie was well endowed. According to him, he found out as much when he was with a promiscuous Asian girl from our college. She informed him that there was only one boy bigger than him on campus. Eddie had mixed feelings about that information. What male wouldn't want to know that he was large? Unless it meant he might lose his penis due to a nasty STD contracted while sleeping with a girl who apparently slept with the entire student body.

Also, Eddie's penis was curved. He thought it was a result of his masturbation obsession. He switched hands when he was fourteen. Eddie did everything with his right hand except masturbate.

Eddie started lifting weights; he filled in and his face cleared. He let his hair grow and discovered hair gel. He upgraded his wardrobe. About a day after all that happened, he met his first wife.

Eddie's first wife was the first really pretty woman he had sex with; the first woman he had sex with sober; the first woman he had sex with more than one time and the first woman he probably gave an orgasm to. Lucky her.

She was also probably the last girl he should have married.

Eddie was pretty sure that he and his first wife were never in love. But pregnancy had a funny way of changing things.

Eddie got married when his wife was six months pregnant. He never lived on his own, "sowed his oats" or got a handle on how to manage an interested female.

Also, Eddie spent the preceding nine plus years feeling unwanted. It started with Andrea Lindstrom, when he was twelve, and lasted until he met his wife at a local bar. Soon after, because life can be a bitch, he noticed a difference when he was around women. All of a sudden, women were interested in what he had to say. They hung around and made themselves available. They gave hints about where they would be and made it clear that they'd like him to be there too.

At the same time, his girlfriend, soon to be his wife, could be more than bitchy. She was older. She'd get mad but wouldn't inform Eddie what it was that upset her. Eddie was left with a choice, start an argument to find out what it was or wait until she got over it. They never worked out anything.

Eddie didn't know any better. He made the mistake of breaking up with his future wife the week before he graduated college and right before he moved in with his parents and started a job search. The breakup made perfect sense when he was surrounded by coeds but turned out to be a disaster. In less than two weeks' time he was desperate to get her back. Unfortunately, by that point, she had moved on and found another boyfriend.

About this time, Eddie molested the giant breasted girl after their movie date. He managed to land a job and started to date one of his sister's friends. She was a pre-med student with red hair and large breasts. But Eddie wanted it all. He wanted big breasts but not at the expense of back fat. Eddie's ex had ruined him with her perfect stomach, ass and legs.

Eddie probably experienced more love from his sister's friend in one month than he did with his future wife in the entire time he knew her. But there was one other item that was working against her besides her back - Eddie's mom. Now, this was all in Eddie's head, but he thought that if he brought a big chested woman home his mom would know he was having sex and disapprove. (Years later, Eddie told his mother about his preference and she thought it was cute.)

A chain of events commenced that ended with Eddie losing his job and his sister's friend, and his wife's pregnancy. Six months later he was married.

Eddie met the bikini separate wearing, big chested girl at the apartment complex swimming pool a month after he was married. His wife was resting in bed, seven months pregnant.

Now here's the cruelest twist of fate. Eddie's wife miscarried. He only married her because he got her pregnant. After the termination of her pregnancy, she went crazy and ended up leaving Eddie.

What was Eddie's biggest regret? Was it losing a child or losing his wife? If you ask Eddie that question today he'll make it clear that it was passing on the girl at the swimming pool.

"I must have gone to that pool every day for a month, until it closed, but I never saw her again."

That was the end of any thought of marriage for Eddie. From that point forward Eddie had only one ambition and that was getting laid.

CHAPTER 16

◄○►

EDDIE BEZZLER WAS USING DECLAN WALKER Wright's ID but couldn't use his credit cards so it would probably be best to stay at independently owned hotels and motels as he made his way south.

I made it to Terre Haute, Indiana and thought it was a good time to find a place to rest. The Statesman Inn looked perfect. It was the type of place that required thick dark curtains to block the headlights of parking cars from periodically illuminating your room.

"How will you be paying for your room, sir?" The man at the front desk asked me.

"Cash."

"That will be eighty dollars."

"Here's a hundred."

He was happy. I was happy. I asked him if there was a nearby bar. I was given two choices: a gentleman's club a half-mile away or a bar and grill a little further along. I wrote down the address of both and headed to my room.

It was exactly what I expected: Two beds with outdated, garish bed covers stained carpet and a yellowing, linoleum-floored bathroom. They really should supply guests with a pair of tongs, to remove the bedcovers. *Are they ever washed?* 'We just changed the bedding and now we're going to seal the clean linen with a quilted petri dish.'

I brushed my teeth and reapplied deodorant and headed out. I drove by the gentleman's club but was too afraid to enter. It looked more like a clubhouse than a bar. Something told me there wasn't a single gentleman in the place. I was nervous that I would be unwarily entering a biker bar. I continued on to the bar and grill and was pleasantly surprised. The place was quite charming, the complete opposite of the gentlemen's club.

I sat at the bar and ordered a beer and a glass of ice water. That was never easy outside of Philadelphia.

"Can I get a glass of wadder?"

"Excuse me?"

"Wadder. A glass of ice wadder?"

"I'm not understanding you, sir?"

Then with much struggle, "Waw-ter... a glass of ice wo-ter."

"Oh, water. Sure, one second."

The bartender served me my beer and ice waw-ter and handed me a laminated menu. I found my bar and grill go to, the French dip, and was quite content on experiencing an uneventful end of my first day on the road.

The next morning, I awoke, opened the curtains that could have been used in a movie theater and realized I was staying at a motel directly across from a large graveyard.

I took a shower and headed out. I drove south on the 41 hoping to locate a small-town diner but all I found was Denny's. I began to notice during my previous day's drive that every small town looked the same. There were the same restaurants and stores, just in different settings.

After my Denny's breakfast I decided to walk to the Larry Bird statue.

Growing up in Philadelphia, I had little appreciation for the man. I was too young to watch him play in his prime but my father talked a lot about him. In the late seventies and early eighties, there was Larry Legend, Magic Johnson and the Sixers. Dr. J was our most famous player but he was past his prime when Larry and Magic started dominating the league. My father told me he didn't appreciate Bird's greatness because he was too busy rooting against him and the hated Celtics. I decided to go see the statue because it was something my dad would have done.

My father was a big sports fan but he would never ask for another man's autograph or wear his jersey. He enjoyed sports because it was a test of a man's limits and a measurement of how someone would perform under pressure. He was equally amazed by an athlete's ability to remain calm in high pressure situations as he was by a spectacular physical feat.

Larry Bird entered the league and didn't seem a bit phased by large crowds and the older, more established players. My father might have despised the Celtics but he respected Larry Bird.

My father was a big fan of my running efforts. He ran himself. We'd discuss training methods; I'd blow his mind recounting some of my college workouts. He couldn't believe we'd run so fast in practice. He spoke a lot about keeping my head straight. He didn't want me to take running too seriously. Not in the sense that I did, taking running more seriously than my schooling. He might have been okay with that. In the sense that the result of any race or practice was insignificant, no matter what some crazed coach might think.

He was constantly telling me to have fun, not stress and that I could quit running any time I wanted to. We might discuss race strategy but it was mostly me explaining what I did or planned to do; he never made suggestions. Before a competition he would try to make me laugh. He wanted me to dream. He would call me "Pre" so I might feel invincible like we imagined Pre felt.

My dad was a dreamer and impractical. He left a lucrative position at an engineering firm for less pay at a different firm because they supported a running club. There, he and his coworkers went on midday training runs and could shower at work. If one of the Philadelphia teams made the playoffs, my dad wasn't going to miss a game, even if it meant leaving work early. He almost lost his job when he called out to attend the Sixers' championship parade in '83.

The size of the Larry Bird statue was in proportion to his legend. It looked to be at least ten feet high. Ten foot tall Larry Bird wearing the short shorts the players wore in the seventies. Even at those dimensions the statue shorts looked less than two feet long.

While I was viewing the statue, a homeless man approached, but he wasn't there for a handout. He was there to pay homage.

"Greatest player ever," he proclaimed.

"One of them," I replied. "Used to be it was Jordan, Magic, Russell, Duncan, if you considered him a power forward, and Bird. But now, LeBron might have moved Bird out of the all-time starting five," I said, expecting an argument.

"You're crazy! LeBron didn't even play college ball. Bird almost lead tiny Indiana State to a national championship."

"Good point. It would have been nice to see LeBron compete in college."

"Wonder where he would have gone."

"I think Ohio State."

This guy didn't seem like the crazy kind of homeless. You can't even talk to those guys. He didn't look like a junkie either. It had to be alcohol. He seemed to be freshly homeless. His clothes were filthy and his hair was dirty and unkempt but not two-years in dirty and unkempt. He looked to be about forty years old but you can never tell with the homeless because they age faster than people who live indoors. His pants looked five sizes too big; he kept them rolled up at the bottom. They hung about three inches above some grimy, strong looking work boots.

"It's starting to cool down," He commented.

"Yep," I replied thinking about how much more important weather was to him than it is to me and how much I bitch about it. "Weather is a big deal to you, isn't it?"

"It can be. Nights can really suck."

"I bet. I would only want to be homeless somewhere warm."

"Should I start walking south?"

"Either that or take a bus."

"There's more competition in the warm cities and I know this town. You from around here?"

"No. I'm from Philadelphia."

"I've been there."

"How about you?"

"What?"

"You from around here?"

"Where else would I be from? You think anyone ends up homeless in Terre Haute if they grew up somewhere else?" He snapped.

"Good point, but I've never been homeless. You'd know more than I would."

"I lose my temper. That's the reason I ended up like this," he said in a completely different tone. He seemed ready to unburden himself.

"Really?"

"Yeah, I fought with my bosses, my wife, my landlord, everybody. I burned every bridge. Now it's just me and my temper."

"That's some problem. At least you recognize it."

"Just did, right now. You asked me the exact same question I asked you and I took issue."

"What are you going to do now?"

"I think I can get some help at the church."

"You're not a drunk?"

"Me? No. I mean, I won't turn a drink down but that didn't put me in this situation."

"What kind of work did you do?"

"I was a mechanic."

"Could you get a job here in town? Sounded like that might be a problem."

"Well, I screwed things up at my brother's shop...Shrock... Sir Thomas... Dusty's..."

"Your brother owns a shop?"

"Yes."

"Younger or older?"

"Older."

"He'll take you back."

"What makes you so sure?"

"Because he's an older brother. Whatever you did, I bet he did far worse when you were kids. I didn't have an older brother but I've heard horror stories from friends that did. Let's go see him. You can take a shower at my hotel beforehand. What's your name anyways? Mine's Declan."

"I'm Rudolph," he said and extended his hand. Rudolph? What a great name. No one named Rudolph should end up homeless.

"Nice to meet you Rudolph." We shook hands. Rudolph's shake was a bit timid but dry.

"You sure? Maybe I should give it a day?"

"No. Come on. No better time than right now."

Rudolf lowered his head in thought and then slowly took a step forward, behind me. When we got to my car, he hesitated. He knew how dirty he was and maybe thought I wouldn't want him to sit down on my new seat cover.

"Don't worry about it. It's a seat cover. It can be replaced," I said, sort of reading his mind.

"Nice car," Rudolf replied without an ounce of sarcasm. "They don't make them like this anymore."

Rudolf and I drove back to my hotel. I got him a room. Paid for a month upfront. He told me what size he was and I went to Old Navy and picked him up some clothes. I took him to a barber shop. Two hours later, old Rudolph was a new man.

We drove over to his brother, Don's place. Don looked younger than Rudolph. He was wearing blue coveralls and gloves made out of grim. As soon as Don saw Rudolph, his eyes teared up. That got Rudolph started. Then I started up, and I didn't even know these guys.

I thought I was going to have to buy Don a new lift or some sort of calibrator to get him to rehire Rudolph but all we had to do was show up.

"Good to see you Rudolph," Don said.

"You too, Don. Sorry about everything," Rudolph replied.

"I don't think I've ever heard those words coming from you," Don said. And a statement like that might have set Rudolph off in the past but he took it in stride.

"I know. I'm going to do my best to change. I can't spend another winter outdoors."

"I can help. Love you brother."

"Love you too."

"Who's this gentleman?" Don asked Rudolph but he was looking me in the eye with his hand extended.

"Hi. I'm Declan. Nice to meet you," I answered and shook Don's hand.

"We met at the Larry Bird statue."

"I guess the Legend lives on," Don proclaimed.

I said my goodbyes and was walking back to my car when Rudolph stopped me.

"Mister, there's something special about you. I don't think you know it yet, but there is," he told me.

"You're the one that's special Rudolph. Good luck to you. Think about the way you felt when you saw your brother tearing up, if you start feeling the anger building inside of you."

"I will. Thank you."

Maybe it was Larry Legend, like Don claimed. But maybe Rudolph was right.

CHAPTER 17

—◄◦►—

I LEFT TERRE HAUTE, JUMPED ON THE 70 and headed towards St. Louis.

As soon as I was on the freeway I started thinking about my family.

When my dad switched firms to devote more time to his hobby, my mom was okay with it. She was a nurse and made enough money to support the family. She was more concerned about my dad's happiness than their bank account. When my father lost his job a year later, she supported him when he went out on his own.

My father started his own business. He would help inventors bring their products to market. My father felt he had a good idea what would sell and what wouldn't and he could help the people with the engineering aspects of their creations. Trouble was, he didn't have the resources to bridge the gap between a good idea and a profit generating business. What inventors need most is money; money for development, production, packaging, marketing… If any of the inventions he was backing sparked interest, the inventor would soon realize that he or she didn't really need any more of my father's help.

171

My dad's business failed and our family was left with a garage full of candle molds, bicycle hangers and reading kits. My dad was an engineer and a mathematician but he was on the downslope of his career. He had difficulty locating new employment. He ended up working for Pennsylvania's Department of Revenue, as an auditor. He wasn't too thrilled by the job or the people he worked with.

My dad was left with a heavy heart. So heavy that he stopped running. He gained twenty pounds and walked around looking like he had lost his best friend. One day, my mom came home with a wrapped box and handed it to my father. He opened it and a puppy jumped out. It was a depression bomb. Boom! Gone was the sadness and self-loathing. My dad and his dog, Pre, became inseparable. He took the dog on long walks, lost the extra weight and made the most out of a job he thought was beneath him.

That experience with my father and my mother's reaction changed me. I wasn't going to let myself be dependent on an employer and would never settle for just any woman. I witnessed how my mother stood by my father and supported him. I had to find the same for myself.

It's only two hundred something miles from Terre Haute to St. Louis. Terre Haute is surrounded by bigger cities, all within a half a day's drive. If I had grown up there, I would have stayed just long enough to say goodbye.

I know something about nearly every city in the world, mostly related to sports. What I know about St. Louis is, it's a smaller city that had trouble supporting an NFL team. I know about the Arch. I know they have a really good baseball team that the Phillies let into the playoffs a few years back and then lost to them in the first round. I know about Stan "the man" Musial because I wondered at his stats on the back of his baseball cards that my father collected. I know about Anheuser Busch, of course. Oh, I know Chuck Berry was born there. Chuck told me that. Well, not Chuck Berry but my friend Chuck. If you wanted to wake my friend Chuck from a coma, just say something disparaging about Chuck Berry.

"Do you know Chuck Berry's only a few years younger than my grandma?" Chuck asked me once. "He still performs and my grandma can't name a single rock song."

When my friend John found out that Budweiser was purchased by a Belgian company, we thought his head was going to explode. When I informed him that Europeans and South Americans drank more beer than Americans, he stopped talking to me for a week.

St Louis is directly west of the Mississippi river so when you hear the statement, "the largest...tallest...fill in the blank west of the Mississippi" that's where you start measuring.

I wrote a paper about the Arch when I was in middle school. I had visited the city during a summer break. St, Louis calls itself, "The Gateway to the West" so an arch didn't require a lot of thought. It was a thirteen million dollar investment in 1965 that has probably paid off one hundred fold. If you consider cities in the Midwest, it's one of the most famous and it's probably because of the arch. I wonder if officials from Kansas City are kicking themselves because they didn't think of it? Oklahoma City, for instance, is twice the size of St. Louis and only has one professional team, the Thunder, and they stole the team from Seattle. St. Louis had three pro teams. St Louis built an arch. Oklahoma City built the world's largest McDonald's.

I left the freeway and made my way west through the downtown area. It had a nice old town feel to it. The streets were much cleaner than the streets in Philadelphia. That holds true in just about every big American city. I don't know why Philadelphia is so dirty. All I know is when I visit a cleaner city, I notice right away.

I was stopped at a red light and was half paying attention, half daydreaming. There was a line of cars turning left around my car onto the road where I was driving. I sort of noticed a boat on wheels pass by, then another odd-looking vehicle. I'm not always the most patient driver, even during the weekend, in the middle of a road trip. I noticed their light turned yellow and expected the line of cars to stop but that didn't happen. The light turned red and the cars kept coming. What the...?! Maybe I didn't know how it was done in St. Louis but a red light is a red light. My light turned green and I was determined to move forward. So I did. I honked, to alert the line of reckless vehicles. I was almost three quarters through the intersection when I noticed a policeman directing traffic. Fortunately for Eddie, the cop had no back up. Just then it hit me. It was a parade. I drove through the middle of a parade. Here I was, pretending to be a wanted fugitive, and I did something as careless as cut through a holiday parade.

I had to be more careful. I quickly exited the city and got back on the freeway. I had to drive through Missouri to reach Oklahoma. I would be traveling from the Gateway Arch to the world's largest golden arches.

CHAPTER 18

—◀◯▶—

HERE'S MY LIFE STORY AS IT pertains to fast and other unhealthy food:

Due to my father's career issues, my family didn't have a lot of money when I was growing up, so we almost never ate out. No pizza nights, no birthday parties at McDonald's and no soda in the fridge. My mom and dad maintained a vegetable garden in the backyard and we ate a lot of whole foods.

Now, don't get the idea that my mother and father were hippie health nuts. My mom permitted the purchase of two packages of cookies per week. My father used to take two cookies and smear butter on one and eat them like a disgusting fat sandwich. He also used to eat the fat I cut off my pork chop along with the fat from his own.

I grew up eating two or three bowls of Chex cereal every morning with healthy scoops of sugar sprinkled on top. I would wash it all down with a big glass of orange juice. For lunch, I packed a sandwich, some chips and bought an ice tea out of a vending machine. Sometime between lunch and dinner I ate between one and two-dozen hard pretzels. For dinner, it could be spaghetti, chicken liver, ham, noodles with corn beef, homemade hamburgers with no bun, always a vegetable, powdered milk until I was sixteen or so and then water. We always had some form of dessert, whether it was the cookies or one of my dad's homemade pies.

Then there was tooth pain, a trip to the dentist… eighteen filings later, a vow to give up sugar.

In my late teens, I started drinking diet soda. I had diet cokes with lunch and every time I bought a slice of pizza or a soft pretzel at the mall. After college, I went through a Whopper faze. I might have six or more each week and always accompanied with fries and a soda.

Then I read Fast Food Nation and watched *Super Size Me*, specifically the bonus footage that was included with the DVD. When you're shown how a Big Mac and fries don't decay in a year's time, why would you ever want to put that in your body? Or if you're on one of those photo blogs and you see how Coke can be used to clean a car battery, why would you want to pour it down your throat?

The interesting thing about my parents is they didn't have a lot of money but didn't go the fast food route, like a lot of other low-income families. My parents' financial situation was a result of illogical decisions made by my father, not from lack of ability or ambition. Stupid people aren't the most successful people and tend to enjoy ignorance. My parents weren't stupid.

My sister took it one step further. She became a vegetarian when she was still in high school, forcing my father to cook two different dinners, one for my mother and me and the other for my sister. My sister is three years older than me. She was quiet and bookish. When I was out playing sports, she was inside reading. My sister is probably the most stubborn person I've ever known. If we fought for control of the only TV set in the household and if I won the battle but used force instead of following the established unwritten rules, she would stand and stare at me for the entire program or until I couldn't take it any longer.

When we were kids, my sister scratched the front of my parents' dresser and sat quiet in her room while I received a corporal punishment administered by my father. I've never let her forget this incident and have told the story to each and every significant other, potential significant other, friend and acquaintance my sister has brought before me.

But I have committed a lifeful of sins: I pushed her into the tub and chipped her front tooth. I killed one of her parakeets by brushing its "teeth" and let another fly out the window. I built a tree fort over top of her secret, quiet place in a maple tree behind our house. I stole the tip money she made while waitressing at a local Chinese restaurant. I set her up with a real dork from work because I could only see her as the snot nosed girl that sat across from me at the breakfast table. I dated one of her friends and treated her so poorly that the girl stopped talking to my sister.

Looking back, it's amazingly self-centered of me to continue to harbor resentment towards my sister for the dresser scratching incident when I'm clearly leading in our jerky behavior competition.

My sister is a web developer, like Chuck. Sometimes they work together on projects. Chuck believes my sister has OCD. It's an ongoing debate between the two of them. My sister has the habit of inventorying everything she did on a particular day, before she falls asleep. It makes her feel productive. I think my mother has the same habit.

"Every night you run through your list. What happens if you accomplish less in a day than you did on a previous day?" Chuck will ask.

"I'm okay with that," My sister will respond. "It's just about giving myself a feeling of accomplishment."

"I doubt you're okay with a shorter list but give me some examples."

"You know, cleaning the house, washing my car, exercising, completing some work project..."

"See? Half of those items aren't accomplishments."

"What are you talking about?"

"Washing your car and cleaning the house are tasks, not accomplishments."

"Sure they are!"

"It's not an accomplishment if you can pay someone else to complete the task for you. You can't pay someone to exercise for you. I guess you could pay someone to complete your work project but only if it was basic work. I could get into that but then we'd be starting a new debate about delegating."

"Whatever. Don't worry about what I do."

It doesn't end there. Two super stubborn people who won't give in.

In case you're wondering, there's never been anything between Chuck and my sister. He treats her like a sister and she treats him like a brother. I'm happy about that because I'd hate for something to happen and we couldn't all remain friends.

I won't let Eddie anywhere near my sister.

Oh, one more item about my sister: My sister's first name is Bevan and her middle name is Sue. My parents let her choose her confirmation name. My sister chose Bevan. So my sister's name is Bevan Sue Bevan. You would think that my parents would have made her choose a different name. Maybe they tried, but my sister can be very stubborn.

* * *

Just outside Oklahoma City is what used to be the world's largest McDonald's. In one of the greatest marketing ideas ever, the restaurant was built like a bridge that spans the freeway. It's impossible to miss. It's the visual equivalent of the ice cream man's incessant music; every kid that sees the approaching arches probably begs his or her parents to stop.

The restaurant straddles the freeway the way an overweight male would straddle a urinal. I had to stop. I wanted to experience firsthand the apex of fast food.

My first thought was that the world would be better off if some foreign country deemed the establishment a weapon of fast destruction and blew it up.

Just suppose that there was another country that had over two hundred years of empirical evidence of the detrimental effects of eating McDonalds and that country decided to rescue the U.S. from its tyranny. In the dark of night, they flew jet fighters overhead and dropped bombs on all the fast food establishments in our country. Of course, the bombing wouldn't be extremely precise so there would be a great deal of collateral damage. Then, the invading country sent in troops to prevent any new fast food restaurants from opening. Would we embrace our liberators? Would this be good use of the other country's resources and the lives of its fallen soldiers?

No way! The whole scenario sounds absurd. What country would be so self-important to think they should dictate how other populations should eat? Many Americans would rise up and battle the other country's troops. Others would establish clandestine burger shops. Years would pass and the anti fast food country would spend billions trying to keep us in check. Many of us would ignore their propaganda and make homemade Whoppers and Big Macs. Finally the other country would give up and go back home. Americans would rejoice and fast food joints would open everywhere. The invading country's economy would suffer for years.

The only parties that would profit would be the companies that supplied the anti fast food country's military and the black market fast food provocateurs.

So there I was, in the fast food mecca, strategically located on one of America's main arteries, in the heart of the Midwest. People scurried in and out of the establishment like enormous ants. Inside was a bit disappointing, though. I was expecting to see a McDonalds times twenty: twenty times the odor, the activity, the waste… but it wasn't much bigger than the McDonald's you would find in a major airport.

I caught a glimpse of the manager. Think about the life of the manager of close to the world's largest McDonald's. Good pay? Yes. But "good pay" does not equal liberating wealth. It usually equals an increased standard of living that's only sustainable with the continuation of employment. Great work experience? Maybe a feather in your cap but unless you're able to break into McDonald's executive team, anything else would be a step down. Rewarding work? Maybe if you focused on helping the kids who were just getting started in the working world. But you'd have to handle the customer complaints, the fact that you're a purveyor of poor health and go home smelling like fried fish every day.

I don't understand why the worst food possible is so popular. It's not even food. It's fake food. Everything they serve is the most highly processed version of food. Since I almost never eat there, if I eat a burger, all I taste is grease and salt wrapped in a puffy manila envelope. Accompany that with indestructible fries; wash it down with a carbonated, chemical cocktail and you have a typical meal at McDonalds.

The only time you're happy about eating it is while you're eating and maybe for five more minutes and then regret. It's not true that McDonald's uses pink goop to make their chicken McNuggets, but they do blend the meat from thousands of chickens to create chicken breast paste. The same thing happens with their burgers. So when nutritionists are recommending you eat food from as close to its source as possible, McDonald's is the opposite of that.

Most people seem more concerned about the quality of gas they pump in their cars than the type of food they shove down their throats. And it's not just people being self-destructive because they feed it to their kids.

The only explanation is that people have made themselves believe that McDonald's is actual food. McDonald's plays along by listing nutritional information on their packaging and in their restaurants. They serve "healthy" alternatives like processed salads, fruits, milk and juices.

As you can tell, I'm not a fan of fast food.

I didn't want to eat at what was no longer the world's largest McDonald's. I'm sure I consumed some calories just by breathing the grease choked air.

My involvement in Eddie's escape was depressing me. So far, I experienced nothing but road hypnosis and poor nutrition. I was on the verge of turning Eddie in. I needed to find a place to spend the night and a decent meal.

CHAPTER 19

—◄○►—

THE RELAX INN HAS TOO GREAT a name to pass up. I had never been to the Relax Inn but I was sure I wouldn't have to engage in any labor during my stay.

Turns out that the Relax Inn is a chain and the guy at the front desk insisted on receiving a credit card. The whole Eddie Bezzler thing was pretty stupid anyway.

So far, this had been a pretty boring trip but I was supposed to be Eddie and Eddie had to lay low and not draw attention to himself. And if you tell me to drive to Tucson, that's what I am going to do. I get tunnel vision and have a hard time relaxing until a task is completed. It's something I've been fighting against for most of my adult life. It sounds like one of those made up personal weaknesses you'd mention in a job interview.

"What's your biggest weakness?"

"I can't relax until I complete my work."

I got it from my mother. She won't rest until she's taken care of every responsibility. She's a good compliment to my father's laid back manner. My mom would go and go and then right before bed, then she'd sit down and drink a beer and eat a couple of pretzels while she read a book. That was the extent of her relaxation.

My mother worked full time, cleaned the house, did the laundry, bought the groceries, washed the dishes and all my father did was cook dinner. There were times when I wondered why my mom stayed with my dad. I didn't want them to divorce but I would have understood if she decided she had enough. Maybe my father calmed my mother down? Maybe without him she wouldn't have had her beer and pretzels.

I had both of them inside me, though. Part of me was go, go, go and then there was this big dreamer chunk. It was sort of embarrassing. I mean, I would never want to reveal the Eddie Bezzler story to Chuck or Eddie. Makes me wonder what went on inside of my father's head. So in this circumstance, I pretended I was a wanted fugitive and didn't take the time to enjoy myself in any of the cities I visited. It was my father dreaming and my mother hurrying him along. Was it my father in me who came up with the rationalization that Eddie needed to lay low or did my mother put those thoughts in my head?

My mother knew how to handle my father. Without her, he'd probably be living in a trailer, surviving on Ramen and running with the Tarahumara. Without my dad, my mother would have been a chain smoking ball of stress. He was a sail and she was the wind; together they were something. I took it one step further and fused the two. I guess that makes me a motor boat. I would never have accomplished what I did without my father's imagination or my mother's drive. Or without my father's math aptitude and my mother's practicality. So my dad wanted to fool around and fantasize and my mother put him on a time schedule.

I asked the guy at the front desk where to go for a beer and dinner and he told me to head downtown. Downtown Vinita was less than a mile away. I decided to walk because of all the driving.

If you're afraid of heights you should move to Vinita, Oklahoma. It's as flat as a table and only a few of its buildings are more than a story.

While I walked down the sidewalk I wondered how much I stood out, or if I stood out at all. Coming from a big city, I assume that everyone in a small town knows each other and that outsiders are monitored. I also feel like I have some special pass because I'm white. I have absolutely no reason for thinking or believing that the citizens of Vinita were on high alert or that they were prejudiced in anyway. In fact, it was prejudicial of me to walk around with those thoughts in my head.

But there's a big difference between prejudice and racism. We're all prejudice and preconception serves a purpose in certain circumstances. People without prejudice could be viewed as naive or innocent. For instance, it wouldn't be wise for a black man to enter a room full of skinheads. So my prejudice regarding small, rural cities made me more aware of my surroundings. I wouldn't walk into a public restaurant and make a nuisance of myself, for instance. I'm going to lay low and be on my best behavior, similar to the way Eddie Bezzler would want me to behave, to avoid capture.

That's why I needed to get out of Vinita. Sorry Eddie. I'm moving forward as Declan. I felt something pulling me west. It was time for me to accept who I was and enjoy myself.

CHAPTER 20

—◁○▷—

T O REACH NEW MEXICO I HAD to drive through the Texas panhandle. There's exactly one attraction along the way - the Cadillac Ranch, in Amarillo, and you can see that from the freeway. It should be called the "Cadillac Farm" because the cars seem to be growing out of the soil. One more thing Texas got wrong.

I drove on, made it through the panhandle and into New Mexico, the "Land of Enchantment." Let me say first, New Mexico's turquoise and yellow license plates were the prettiest plates ever made. Second, NASA most definitely could have faked the lunar landings by using New Mexico as a backdrop.

I planned to spend the night in Albuquerque but couldn't find a vacancy. Albuquerque was in the middle of its famous balloon festival. It was another hundred miles to Gallup, which seemed an insignificant distance after driving for more than two days.

Driving from Albuquerque to Gallup, at night, is like driving in a tunnel. There were times during the drive when I felt claustrophobic. Headlights from oncoming cars were blinding. I tried using my high beams but had to be more conscious of the other cars; turning the beams off and back on again became a chore. For all I knew, I drove past a herd of buffalo, space aliens and a few murder scenes. When I finally saw the bright lights of Gallup, it felt like I was on a night flight, descending into a city.

I pulled up to the El Rancho Hotel, which promised the "charm of yesterday" and the "convenience of tomorrow." It was right on historic Route 66. Since I was no longer traveling under an assumed name, I decided to upgrade my stays.

What were some of the El Rancho's futuristic conveniences?

Well, they had free Wi-Fi, a 24-hour front desk, a seasonal pool, three floors and an elevator. Breakfast was available, for a surcharge, but there was free parking. I can't imagine you'd ever have to pay to park in Gallup.

"How many keys? The front desk person asked.

It was just me so I replied, "Just one." Then I thought about how many times, especially when I was tired, the card keys didn't work. But then thought that I was being silly and stuck to my answer.

I rode the slow elevator up to the third floor and walked what seemed like two football fields across vibrant carpet, to my room. Sure enough, the door wouldn't open. 'Do I leave my bag? No, someone might take it. Try again. Fuck! Still doesn't work.'

Back at the front desk, "Try to keep the key separate from your phone," was the desk clerk's advice.

Waking up in New Mexico is like waking up on the sun. New Mexico has to be the darkest place at night and the brightest place during the day. If you want to experience waking up in New Mexico, go to a matinee movie on a sunny day.

Gallup calls itself America's Most Patriotic Small Town. It's also home of the Fu King Chinese Buffet.

Gallup, population twenty thousand, has a Walmart Superstore. So do its two neighbors, Grants, New Mexico and Winslow, Arizona. That's three superstores servicing less than forty thousand potential customers. I'm not going to criticize Walmart and accuse it of predatory pricing and driving small mom and pop shops out of business. How could I? I made my millions in technology. Do you know the number of jobs technology has eliminated?

Often the internet is held to blame for the struggling newspaper business. But all the internet did was create a better delivery system. When you think about it, there's nothing sillier than printing papers and then hand delivering them to readers. Forget the fact that you're asking the news cycle to pause itself for six or more hours, newspaper publishing requires an amazing amount of resources for something that has such a short shelf life.

Newspapers might have flourished on the internet. Large city papers still could. Why haven't they? Two reasons: First, it's a lot easier to charge premium rates for advertising when it's difficult to determine its effectiveness. With the internet, advertisers can easily track the results of their ads. After reviewing those results many companies went in a different direction. Second, thanks to Craigslist, one of the newspapers' main revenue generators – classified advertising - disappeared completely. Nothing beats free.

Consider all the jobs Craigslist has eliminated. And I'm not just talking classified ad sales. Dozens of jobs per major paper, around the world, have been eliminated by a company with fewer than fifty employees.

In my lifetime, we went from almost everyone purchasing a newspaper to almost no one. That affects more than just the people that worked for the newspapers. It affects newsstands, convenience stores, everyone involved in the delivery system, including mechanics that maintained the delivery vehicles and the companies that manufactured them.

Walmart is despised by many of the people that adore Google. But Google's span of destruction is much wider than Walmart's.

The phone companies used to make millions selling listings. If you wanted your business listed in the white pages and directory information, you had to purchase a business phone line. Business lines are more expensive than their residential counterparts. The phone features on business lines were more expensive than residential phone features, so are the installation charges. If your business operated in a densely populated area, there were more directories to be listed in, all at a cost.

Before Google became popular, people could earn a living wage answering the phone and looking up phone numbers for customers. If you were too lazy to open up your phone book or someplace where one wasn't available, you might pay close to a dollar for information that Google provides today, free of charge.

If you have no love for the Phone Company, consider its employees. The Phone Company was one place where just about anyone could earn a decent living. I worked at the Phone Company and found out that it was a haven for single moms. Phone companies made large profits but they shared the wealth. Compare that to Apple. Based on revenue per square inch, Apple stores are the most profitable retail operations in existence, but the last time I checked their store employees averaged twelve bucks an hour.

The Yellow Pages was another place an average person could earn some serious scratch. A successful salesperson could make six figures or more selling Yellow Page advertising. Those jobs are all gone, along with just about every other position at the Yellow Pages.

Google offers a more efficient way to reach potential customers. If you're reading an article on a website, you're probably not thinking about making a purchase. If you see an ad to the side, it might grab your attention but you're not necessarily in shopping mode. But when you're searching for a term in Google, especially when your entry includes words like "deals", "providers" or "service" you're actively looking to make a purchase. What type of advertising do you think makes more sense to a business? But Google doesn't produce anything. All its content is user generated. All they did was create a meeting place and directory. Google doesn't need to pay writers or producers. They don't even need to employ salespeople or order-processors because everything is automated.

What jobs did Google create?

A great number of tech jobs; most of which are out of reach to the average person.

Indirectly, Google created a need for web developers, internet marketers and search engine optimizers.

But Google looks at optimizers the same way store owners view shoplifters. Google routinely changes its algorithms in an effort to "improve search results" and frustrate optimizers.

By reducing the effectiveness of optimizers, Google has effectively reduced the value of owning a website, resulting in fewer web developers.

Technology has led to job reduction in other areas as well.

Easy Pass is replacing tollbooth operators. Grocery store clerks are being replaced by self-service technology. Online video streaming killed Blockbuster Video. MP3 nearly killed the music industry. ITunes is working on eliminating the record store jobs that the big box stores weren't able to get to. E-Commerce has reduced the number of insurance and travel agents. Web development has hurt the printing industry. Wikipedia helped eliminate the encyclopedia industry.

There was a time in the late nineties and early two thousands when any decent sized company had a full time IT person on staff. IT training was sought after. That made sense because businesses needed to keep pace with the changing technology. But as technology advanced it became more dependable and easier to manage. The world went from premise based to cloud based technology. IT became an outsourced service. As IT people became more efficient, the ratio of businesses to IT people needed decreased. Now, one IT consultant can effectively service ten to twenty businesses.

Where does all the displaced labor end up? Working at Walmart?

What bothers me about Walmart is it behaves like a frugal couple when the check arrives at a dinner party. A lot of companies are acting that way. These companies produce a multitude of uninsured employees who barely make enough to survive. The workers can't contribute much to the economy and become everyone else's responsibility.

Walmart continues to push their suppliers and vendors. Those companies have to lower their prices, which results in decreased revenue and profits. Eventually, these companies reduce their payrolls, as well. The result - a percentage of the population that can't afford to shop anywhere but Walmart.

CHAPTER 21

—◄○►—

I ATE BREAKFAST AT EARL'S RESTAURANT WHICH was located next to a Pizza Hut and across the street from the Hong Kong restaurant. It was an old fashioned restaurant that served breakfast and Mexican food all day. I think every restaurant in Gallup serves Mexican food all day, even Pizza Hut and the Hong Kong restaurant.

Today I'd be entering Arizona, which despite its conservative politics and veiled racism is one of my favorite states. White people relocate to Arizona and take issue with the brown people; they think they're taking over their state. Never mind that the area that became Arizona was once part of Mexico.

I was going to write out a list of reasons of why I liked Arizona. Items like the weather, the lack of traffic, the cost of living... But because I was born in Philadelphia, singing the praises of another city is similar to rooting for the Cowboys.

Most Pennsylvanians never lived anywhere else. If you tell them about other cities and how those cities are different, they think you're criticizing their state and become defensive. Philadelphians got excited when The Foodery opened up in town and they could buy singles. But a single beer is at least two fifty, which is fifteen dollars a six pack. In Arizona, I'd pay less than that for a twelve-pack at the grocery store. See? I have to stop doing that. Everyone in town was excited about the Foodery, so I have to keep my mouth shut.

Say you're hanging around with some Philadelphians and one of them starts complaining about the humid weather and all the bugs, that's not an invitation to inform the group that the air is dryer in Arizona and bug free. Or if your Philly friend expresses frustration because he or she just spent an hour traveling eight miles on the Schuylkill "Expressway", that person did not ask you to inform them of how wide the highways are in Phoenix. Pennsylvanians can't make their roads wider or air less humid or buggy. Any ideas that I come up with to improve the place are just tweaks anyway - like changing the timing of the traffic lights or adding a turning lane here and there. My tweaks aren't going to make a big difference. I guess the reason I get frustrated with Pennsylvanians is that they love to complain but they have zero intention of moving or changing anything. It's like they're driving an old Chevrolet Celebrity and bitch about it every day but don't look to buy a new car.

Winslow, Arizona was made famous by a slightly above average Eagles song. But Winslow is a dump. Ever get a zit on your nose? Do you know the feeling? It doesn't matter how healthy the rest of your skin looks or if you're having a great hair day, when you look in the mirror, all you can see is the blemish. Well, Winslow is the opposite of that. Winslow is like a face full of acne and a perfect, zit free nose. Right in the center of rundown Winslow is a jewel called the La Posada Hotel.

The La Posada was built by the railroad industry when it was flush with cash. It's still operating as an Amtrak railroad station.

They spared no expense when they built the La Posada. Every square inch, inside and out is magnificent. But the surrounding area is a mess. Maybe the hotel isn't as nice as I think it is. Maybe it's like a somewhat pretty girl surrounds herself with homely friends?

I needed to take a break from all my driving and decided to rest up at the Posada. "La" is "the" in Spanish and here I was writing "the La Posada". That's like saying "the the Posada". That's what happens when white people talk and write about places with Spanish names. Another example is The Hotel Del, in Coronado, California. "Del" is "the", so if you say "the Hotel Del" you're saying "the Hotel The".

I know this because I dated a girl who was born in Mexico. She's Mexican and it's okay to call her that because that's what she is. The politically correct people get nervous calling someone Mexican because not every Hispanic or Latino person originates from Mexico and someone from Spain, for example, would get upset if you called him or her "Mexican". I learned that firsthand when I kept calling a Spaniard, Mexican. He got upset and let me know. After that experience I was afraid to say "Mexican food". But some white people take it too far. A coworker once asked me with a straight face, "Does your girlfriend mind that you call her Mexican?"

Now, this is one of the great things about being rich. I don't care about the cost of a room or room service and I don't have to worry about how long I stay, because I'm not going to miss any work.

"Is this still a working train station?" I asked the gentleman helping me at the front desk.

"Yes sir. You can catch an Amtrak here and it will take you almost anywhere. The next stop west is Williams. From Williams you could hop on a train to the Grand Canyon."

"Really? Where can I buy a ticket?"

That was it. I was headed to the Grand Canyon.

Road trips sound great until you drive for six straight hours, stop at a gas station, attempt to stand and can't feel your legs. They sound great until you've eaten nothing but road meals for two days. They sound great until your windshield becomes a bug crime scene. They sound great until your butt becomes so sensitive it hurts to sit on your wallet.

It wasn't boredom or loneliness that made me give up on my road trip. I don't get that way. Most of the time, I'd rather be alone. And I'm never bored. I get lost in my mind. People used to ask me if I got bored when I ran long distance. I felt sorry for those people. Imagine boring yourself.

I wasn't sure if I should return to Winslow after my trip to the Canyon. I was pretty sure I didn't want to but didn't know what to do with the car.

There are two types of trips: round and one-way. When you start a round trip, you know when you'll be returning. Two days into a round trip and you start focusing on how many days you had left. One-way trips are much more exciting.

Eliminating the car would require more improvisation. I knew how to make it to Williams, but wasn't sure after that. When I wanted to leave the Grand Canyon... I had no idea. All I possessed was the universal key - money.

Screw the car. But I didn't want to just leave it somewhere. I'm the kind of person that likes to give away an extra game or movie ticket instead of selling or letting it go unused. I also like to steer someone towards a parking meter with surplus time. Giving the car away would be a lot trickier. I wanted to give it to some kid but how would that work? A young man shows up at home with a new car; what's he going to say to his parents? That it was from some random dude? The key would be to spot a father and son or daughter pulling into a car lot and offering it to them. But if I did that, I'd upset the car dealer.

I pulled into the first car dealership I saw, a place called Payless. I found the owner. He was an older gentleman that wore one of those bolo ties that you'd expect a business person to wear in Winslow.

"I want to sell my car. How much will you give me for it?"

"Well, I'll need to get my mechanic to take a look but you know these old cars don't carry much value."

"You kidding me? This here's a classic," right away I started talking like the guy or the way I thought the guy would speak, because we just started talking, so I really didn't know.

"Maybe to someone with some money or who knows how to work on cars, but to people in this neck of the woods, it could be more trouble than it's worth."

I took a look around to see where exactly the woods were. These guys are amazing. I was positive the car was worth something but after listening to his explanation, I was ready to give it away.

"Well, can you have your mechanic take a look?"

"Sure will. Can I get you a cup of coffee or some water?"

"Water would be nice."

"Gladys, can you bring this gentleman a bottle of water?"

Had I known that Gladys was going to be the one fetching my water, I might have declined.

I sat quiet for fifteen minutes. I knew what I wanted to do but needed a third party. Just then, a dad and his teenage son walked into the dealership. It was meant to be.

They were Hispanic. The son looked like he had done some work in his life.

"Folks have you been helped?" asked the bolo wearing salesman.

"We're just looking, thank you," the son answered for the father.

Bolo let them alone. Since it was the son that answered, I don't think the father spoke English.

A younger employee walked in the showroom and handed Bolo a piece of paper. It was my estimate.

"Okay. The good news is the car is in decent shape. I could offer you four thousand?"

The Pontiac, it turned out, was not one of my best investments.

"Four thousand?! I paid more than twice that amount less than a month ago?"

"Why you fixin to sell it then?"

"I was going to drive it across country but decided to take a train to the Grand Canyon instead."

Very sympathetic. So now he knew I could afford pay more than eight thousand for a temporary car.

"How much do you think you could sell a car like that for?"

"Well, like I told you. The only people that would be willing to pay a premium for it is maybe a mechanic or someone with a lot of money, and those types don't tend to take up residence in Winslow. I'd be lucky to get five thousand for it."

I knew that was a lowball figure but I got the information I was looking for.

"I'll tell you what. I'll pay you twenty five hundred in cash to sell the car to that father and son over there for one dollar."

Maybe he was working me and could have easily doubled his money on my car, but I got him to volunteer a potential one thousand dollar profit. There's no way he could turn down my offer.

"We don't even know if they want your car."

"Call them over. Let's work out the deal together."

"I guess, but you're doing the talking."

We sat with the father and son and I explained the offer, to the son in English and then he translated for his father. When the father heard the price, he thought the son was mistaken and looked our way and said, "One dollar?"

"Si," I replied.

The kid's smile was as big as a license plate. We had a deal. I had to wait for everything to be finalized. When it was all over, I handed Bolo a stack of twenties.

"You know, that felt good," he proclaimed with a smile slightly smaller than the kid's.

It did feel good.

CHAPTER 22

—◄○►—

T HE TRAIN FROM WINSLOW TO WILLIAMS ran mostly
    parallel to Interstate 40, which replaced Route 66 as the
passageway between Albuquerque and Flagstaff. Route 66, like
Winslow, is something that got its fame from a rock n roll song. If
you stand on the corner of Route 66 in Winslow you'll enter some
sort musical time warp.

It was ninety miles to Williams. There wasn't much to see between
Winslow and Williams. Flagstaff was the only city we passed by.
Flagstaff is hardly a city. It's mostly a college town and a summer
getaway for overheated Phoenicians.

Everyone on the train was on vacation. I'm pretty sure that no
one commutes to Williams from Winslow. It was mostly families.

It would be interesting to know how much money the Grand
Canyon has generated over the years. Not just for the Federal Government, that manages the park, but all the nearby cities and businesses
that are connected in some way. Take Williams, Arizona. That city
calls itself the "Gateway to the Grand Canyon". If you were traveling
from California, you'd pass through Williams to reach the Canyon. If

you were coming up from Phoenix, you'd either go through Williams or Flagstaff. I'd recommend Flagstaff because the drive is a hundred times prettier. But you have to drive to the Grand Canyon (unless you travel by Helicopter). You can take a train, but then you would still travel through Williams. Most people drive because it's a family destination. You load the kids in the car and all their junk and then camp in the Canyon or stay at one of the local hotels. So Williams exists because of the Grand Canyon and it's sixty miles away.

There are hotels inside and outside of the Canyon. If you're more fortunate, you stay at a hotel inside Grand Canyon Village. Otherwise, you have about a twenty minute commute, to and from the Canyon. With a permit, you can camp in one of the Village's campsites.

My first experience with the Grand Canyon was with my mom and sister, and we camped on the South Rim. Since then, I've done everything but reside in one of the hotels inside the park.

The Canyon is a magical place that everyone should see at least once in their lifetime, but it has a dark side as well. I read a book that was two inches thick and four hundred pages long that detailed all the fatalities that have occurred inside the park. Some fell accidently; there have been suicides and murders; but a number of people perished because they underestimated how difficult it can be to hike in the Canyon. People, who were unaware of its extreme temperatures, hiked too far down and didn't take the proper precautions, have made the monument their final resting place.

People associate death with Mount Everest but three times as many people have died in the Grand Canyon. People train to climb Everest; they hire guides and have Sherpas pack their gear and fix climbing ropes. In comparison, tourists in boat shoes and pumps, carrying bottles of soda, enter the Canyon like it's an underground shopping mall.

It could be seventy degrees at the rim and one hundred and twenty at the bottom. So if you're up top and get it into your head that you want to do some real hiking; you start barreling down the trail, and it seems like a real breeze because you're going down a steep grade. The trouble is, every step you make going down is a harder step and a half coming back up. And even though it feels easy to hike down, it puts a strain on your muscles. Then you have to consider the novice factor. The Canyon is a tourist attraction. Tourists aren't necessarily world class athletes or understand the finer points of extreme hiking. They don't wear the proper foot gear or clothing; they don't pack enough water; then they get excited, over extend themselves and require a helicopter rescue or don't make it back at all.

And don't blame the park rangers. If the Canyon was a beach and the rangers were lifeguards and tourists were swimmers, then the beach would be ten miles wide, the lifeguards would be outnumbered, one thousand to one and the swimmers would do dopey things like taking selfies with sharks and swimming a mile out into the ocean before turning around and attempting to make it back to the shore. People pretend to fall in the Canyon and then fall for real. People taking photos, take one step back too far, fall and no one finds out if they were able to capture the shot they were hoping for. And novices walk five miles down a steep mountain and are overwhelmed by the heat and exertion and are at someone else's mercy as to whether they live to tell about it.

After visiting the Canyon with my mother and sister, I considered moving to the area and becoming a ranger, but I'm glad I didn't. Sure I would have been working outside in one of the most beautiful settings in the world. But I would also be dealing with excited dopes, day in and day out, and one experience of witnessing a child die of exposure would have been too many.

* * *

This time, I was going to do the Canyon in style. If it was possible, I was going to bribe my way into an open room in one of the hotels on the rim and stay there as many days as possible.

The El Tovar is right on the rim. For about four hundred and fifty a night, I was able to book a suite for the week. My suite was the only room they had available. There's a slim chance of booking a room in the Canyon on a whim. I imagine many fathers have been put to the test by their family members visiting the Canyon for the first time. Once you're there, you never want to leave. When you realize you can actually stay in a hotel situated directly on the rim, the desire to do so must be great. But just asking requires nerve. You'd probably feel the same way you'd feel if you were asking a clerk at a toy store, on the day before Christmas, if they had *the* fad toy in stock. To summon up the courage to ask and then hear that there was a room available would get your heart racing. Of course the room wouldn't be a reasonably priced vacancy. Most people can't afford four hundred and fifty dollars a night. The kids would get all excited and then daddy would have to bring them back to earth. "Sorry kids." Man, it must suck to be a parent.

I wasn't sure if I was going to hike the canyon or just soak it in. I did know that I'd been wearing the same clothes for the last few days. It was time to splurge at the Grand Canyon General Store.

The General Store looked the same way it did when the Brady kids vacationed in the Canyon back in the seventies. There were probably fifty varieties of the popular "I hiked the canyon" t-shirt and since I had hiked the canyon I bought a couple of those. They don't have any regular duds so I had to buy a bunch of hiking type apparel. You know, long pants that unzip into shorts, that sort of thing. So basically, I would have clean clothes but would be walking around looking like a dork.

I went back to my room and turned my phone on for the first time in about a week.

My family had gotten used to me disappearing. It used to freak them out but not so much anymore. You can't really disappear if you remain tied to your phone.

I received at least a dozen "where are you?" text messages and half as many "where are you?" emails. Thankfully, there was no emergency or trouble back home.

I sent my old clothes to the laundry and tried on some of my canyon gear. After looking at myself in the mirror, I considered locking myself in my room for as long as it took to receive my clothes back laundered.

I went down to the hotel bar and ordered a draft. The girl sitting next to me took a look and said, "Nice shirt."

"I ran out of clean clothes. There's not much to choose from at the general store."

"I was in there. I saw some better options."

She was somewhat of a ball buster.

"You're just jealous."

"Oh yeah? Anyone who's taken one step on one of the trails has 'hiked the canyon'."

"Good point. I'm Declan," I said as I extended a hand.

"Alexis. Nice to meet you."

Alexis had dark hair, tan skin and green eyes. She had a cute little flower, the size of a dime, tattooed on her neck, near her hairline. Her hair was pulled back by the sunglasses resting on the top of her head. She was wearing jeans, sandals with a heel and a gauzy shirt that you could sort of see through. She had a few leather bracelets on her left wrist and a small, silver watch. She had straight white, teeth and I could see a small speck of chewing gum poking out between two of her molars.

"Here on vacation?" I knew it was a silly question.

"No, the government sent me. They're considering shutting down the place."

She was a real cut up.

"Probably a good idea. It's a bit much to maintain."

Alexis offered me a courtesy chuckle.

"What are you drinking?"

"Beer." Alexis's beer glass had a dark-pink lipstick stain towards the top where she was drinking. The lipstick stain was a perfect match for her polished nails.

"You're a real talker, aren't you?"

"Didn't know you wanted to get all technical about it," she replied with a cute smile that displayed a dimple on her right cheek.

Her scent was amazing. I guess you could ask a woman what fragrance she's wearing and after she informed you which one, you could say, "Oh, it smells terrific" but what are you going to do with that information? You're not going to buy it and spray it on yourself. You could buy it and give it to someone, but probably wouldn't have the same smell. Mostly you just ask because you're hoping to extend your time with the woman, basically until you can determine whether or not she likes you.

"The type of beer a person drinks can say a lot."

"Oh, yeah?"

"Yes. For instance, if you drink Bud, Corona or Heineken, you're predictable and a little boring. If you drink Miller High Life, you probably don't care what others think. If you drink light beer, you might be vain or lack taste. If you're a woman and drinking Guinness or an IPA, watch out."

"You can tell it's not Guinness. You get more for your money with IPAs."

"Better watch out," I mumbled. "Where are you from?"

"San Francisco. You?"

"Philly."

Philly is actually a good place to say you're from. It's more metropolitan than cities like Denver or Cincinnati; it doesn't sound as serious as New York City or Washington D.C; it's a big city with a lot of character. You tell someone that you're from Philadelphia and they think you're interesting.

"Haven't been there."

"Lucky you. Not too many reasons to leave San Francisco."

"I like it."

The reason there are so many gays in San Francisco is because it's so beautiful there. Any nice area, the gays find out about and take it over. They usually make it even nicer. And they can afford the expensive areas because they're not paying for kids and college, all that sort of stuff.

"Seriously, what are you doing here at the Canyon?"

"You tell me first."

"I was driving across country and got sidetracked."

"Oh yeah? Your reason has a lot more potential than mine. I'm here with my sister and her kids."

"My car broke down in Winslow. I sold it and took a train here."

"Where were you headed?"

"Mexico. I'm running from the law."

"Really? How exciting."

"Easy for you to say. I don't have a moment of peace; always looking over my shoulder; worried about showing up on the news..."

"What did you do?" she asked in a whispery voice.

"Nothing violent. Embezzlement."

"Then you can pay for my beer."

Just then, three little kids came running up to her. "Tia!" they shrieked.

"I have to go. Hopefully I'll see you around. Are you staying in the hotel?"

"Yes, under an assumed name. Hope to see you again, as well."

I did hope that I would see her again. I hadn't felt that way in years. I wanted to ask her for her number but decided to play it cool. I don't know how many times I played it cool and never saw the woman again, though.

CHAPTER 23

—◄○►—

NOW INSTEAD OF ENJOYING THE CANYON I was obsessed with Tia Alexis. It was early on in my stay, so at least I had that going for me. I became consumed with my appearance. I was very happy when I my clothes came back from the laundry.

It is very difficult to date "normal" women when you maintain my lifestyle. Unless I found the female me, the woman would have responsibilities that she couldn't neglect without consequences. My way of life can be very addictive. Just a sample, and almost anyone would be ready to dump everything. But then that person would become my responsibility. I have to be really sure. My other option is to try to go about my business and see the woman whenever it's convenient, and that never works. If I were selfish, I wouldn't care. I'd seduce a woman and then let her work things out.

I had to get my mind off of Alexis. I decided to do something I hadn't done before. I've backpacked to the bottom of Canyon, camped and hiked back up, on two separate occasions. I've also hiked to the bottom and back up in a single day. The time I did that, I took the traditional route, down South Kaibab and up Bright Angel. This time, I wanted to make the same hike in the opposite direction.

209

No big deal, right? If you think that, you never did any serious hiking in the Canyon. The reason the recommended route is down Kaibab and up Bright Angel is because there's no drinking water on Kaibab and the trail is much steeper. It's about seven miles down Kaibab and nine and a half miles up Bright Angel. There's drinking water on Bright Angel and it's a more gradual climb.

I wanted to hike down Bright Angel because the last few miles of that trail are excruciating. It has nothing to do with the level of difficulty. It has everything to do with the number of dopes you run into when you're tired and irritable. Bright Angel is the tourist trail.

If Kaibab was a set of stairs, Bright Angel would be a wheelchair ramp. The reason Bright Angel is two and a half miles longer is because it's less direct and there are more switchbacks. The last couple of miles can feel more like a long line at at an amusement park, and the same type of people you'd find in line would be on Bright Angel.

Then there are the mule trains. Watching a mule ascend the trail is amazing. If you ever hiked down Kaibab and been passed by a train heading in the opposite direction, you can't believe something so big can climb so effortlessly. But when you're hot and exhausted, the mules are the last thing you want to experience. They stink, leave pools of urine and you're not supposed to walk past them. If the guide has a train stopped and is giving a talk about this or that, you're expected to stop and wait. That shouldn't bother me but it does. I'm busting my hump to make it up the trail, some lazy asses are taking a joy ride and I have to wait?

I despised the last few miles of Bright Angel so much that I haven't wanted to hike the Canyon. Then I thought of reversing the route. It would be more extreme. Seven miles straight up with only the fluid I could carry. I would experience peak temperatures during the most challenging part of my hike. If I fucked up, I could become a headline: "Tech Millionaire Dies While Hiking the Canyon."

My first stop would be back to the General Store to purchase hiking boots (one up from my normal size ten), sunglasses, a dorky hat (to shade my head) and number of different hydration devices.

Why did I buy size eleven hiking boots when I wear size ten? Good question. Because when you hike down a steep, nine mile trail, your feet tend to push forward and if there's less room in the toe, you can end up with a couple of blackened toenails. That and your feet swell when you hike in the high temperatures. If you ever decide to hike down the Canyon, tie your boots extra tight near the top of your laces. Doing so helps prevent your feet from sliding forward into the front of your boots.

I wanted to start early. I woke up at five, ate breakfast and was on my way. No one knew I was making my hike. If I ran into problems, I would become irrational and most likely leave the trail. I would wander off into the wilderness, never to be seen again. (that's how it happens) Since I hadn't replied to any text messages or email, no one knew where I was. The only evidence would come from my credit card statement.

I wasn't worried though. I built up a great deal of endurance from my running days. Also, my high school coach wouldn't let us drink water during practice. From that experience, I evolved into a human camel.

During the first part of my hike, I felt like a genius. It was cool and there was no one on Bright Angel. I reached Indian Gardens and was through the most dreaded part of my hike in less than two hours. The next five miles would be the highlight of my trip.

The temperature climbed as I descended the trail. The sky was clear and the air was dry. I made sure to drink continuously. When you pee, you want your pee to be almost clear, like water. Drinking had to be as routine as breathing and it doesn't help to preserve your fuel. The people that had problems only started drinking after experiencing symptoms of dehydration. At that point it can be too late. That's why kids have trouble; they get too excited and unless their parents are monitoring, they don't drink enough water.

The section of the Bright Angel trail, from the Indian Gardens to the Colorado River is one of my favorite places on earth. Only partly because of its beauty. Mostly because of the solitude. There are thirty-three campsites in Bright Angel campground, so the number of people residing there tops out around one hundred, and not all of them hike out at the same time. There are cabins in Phantom Ranch but almost all of those people are mule riders. Very few day hikers make it past Indian Gardens. Also, no mules are permitted past the Tonto Trail. At most you have a hundred hikers, at any given time, spread out over a five mile section of trail. That's about one person per football field of space. But people usually hike in groups, so the spacing is greater. In all my time on that section of trail, I've seen fewer than a dozen others.

When you're descending the trail, the river is your focal point. Because of the Canyon's scale, the river seems closer than it actually is. Everything does. You'd think it would be the opposite. Scale is right up there with heat and gradient when you're considering the Canyon's challenges. If you found yourself in trouble, you could become disheartened by your lack of progress.

When you reach the end of Bright Angel you cross the Colorado River on the Silver Bridge. The bridge connects the trail to a path that leads to the Bright Angel campground and Phantom ranch. That bridge was built in the sixties and is part of a pipeline that delivers drinking water from the North to the South Rim. All the materials that were used to construct the bridge and its neighbor, the Black Bridge, were transported by man and mule. Crossing either bridge isn't for the faint of heart because the walkway is grating and you can see all the way down to the river below. Before the two bridges existed adventurers crossed the river inside a metal cage attached to a cable. Using that method, only one mule could cross at a time.

The Colorado River is the reason the Grand Canyon exists. The Canyon is a result of an erosion problem left unchecked for millions of years. The river's current is extreme and temperature frigid. The river water is so cold because it originates from the base of the Glen Canyon Dam. It's the water from the bottom of the lake. If you ever swam in a deep lake and submerged twenty feet down or so, the water temperature drops considerably. Also, all the creeks feeding the river originate from melted ice and snow.

The floor of the Canyon, especially in summer time, is made up of extremes. Intense heat and sun and chilly, rushing water. The climate is equivalent to Phoenix. I camped down there one time when the thermometer read one hundred and twenty-two degrees. All I wanted to do was soak my tired feet in the creek. I shouldn't have packed a sleeping bag, because it was too hot to use.

A popular destination at the base of the Canyon is Phantom Ranch. To make it there, you walk along the creek that separates the trail from the Bright Angel Campground. Phantom Ranch consists of a group of cabins and a mess hall. The hall is open to the public. Every night they serve steak and stew. You can buy cans of beer and other supplies. All the provisions and resulting trash, are transported by mule train.

Inside the hall are rows of communal tables. Its visitors are like the United Nations of hikers and campers. The first question asked is "Where are you from?" The answer could be anywhere in the world.

The Ranch has its own post office and mail is stamped with the "Mailed by Mule" Phantom Ranch postmark.

Inside the dining area, I spotted an open seat next to a group of three. They were two men and a woman, probably in their late twenties. The woman was blond and striking. The men were just average.

"Hi. Mind if I join you?" I asked.

"No, not at all. Please sit down," one of men replied with a German accent.

"Where are you guys from?" I asked.

"Austria," the other male replied. "What about you?"

"I'm from Philadelphia."

"Ahhh, Phillleeee!" the first male exclaimed with a smile.

I wondered what was the nature of their relationship. I considered asking but thought better of it.

"Are you all staying here at the ranch?"

"Camping tonight. Tomorrow, we're hiking up Bright Angel. You?"

"I just came down Bright Angel. I'm taking a break and then I'm going to hike up Kaibab."

"You're going in reverse order," the girl said. How cool, she knew.

What's to say she wasn't the woman of my dreams? I'm not saying I felt that way but talk about your chance encounters. We were from different continents and happened to meet at one of the most remote parts of the country. Maybe the Canyon was my Lost Island? All I had to do was go there and all my troubles would disappear.

Once I knew they were Austrian, I analyzed their hair styles, clothing and equipment, to see if any of it was different. I was always doing that. If I was watching a foreign film, I would be fixated on the background, trying to spot an odd looking doorknob or coat hanger.

"What's that in your bottles?" I asked. It looked like dirty water.

"It's diluted tea," the woman replied.

Interesting, Americans considered tea a diuretic. I was forcing down warm water and sports fuel.

"Is this your first time hiking the canyon?"

"Yes! It's truly astonishing."

It made me proud to hear a foreigner praise an American landmark, like I had something to do with its creation.

"This is my fifth visit. Every time, I see something new."

"I bet," the woman replied. "If I lived in the States I would want to come every year."

That's usually the way you feel when you visit the park. Every time I'm there, I ponder the possibilities. Perhaps two or three months of exploration? Maybe a permanent relocation? Without a partner it would probably get lonesome. I could ask the Austrian?

"Well if you're looking for a sponsor?" Right after I finished the sentence, I wish I had kept my mouth shut. For all I knew the woman was with one of the two men. There was silence and then the Austrians said their goodbyes and got up to leave. As they headed out the woman looked back and smiled. Maybe there was a connection? I'll never know.

After lunch and some rest, I began the most challenging part of my hike. I'd been at it for over five hours and still hadn't started the hardest part.

Here's what I think when it comes to attempting challenging pursuits: If the endeavor doesn't seem too severe, treat it otherwise. Maybe I wasn't climbing the North Face of Eiger, I could still pretend. If anyone ever died while attempting something, than that something is life threatening. If you're engaged in any endurance type activity, your brain is half your battle. It helps to dream. If you're running, imagine you're racing in the Olympics. If you're climbing, pretend you're Tenzing Norgay.

The largest hydration pack I could find at the general store was a hundred ounces. That's a little less than a gallon of water. I also purchased a twenty-four ounce bottle that I could attach to a pack strapped around my waist. That gave me a little less than a gallon of fluid for a seven-mile hike. That's plenty for almost any other seven-mile stretch. But I'd be climbing roughly five thousand feet. If that doesn't sound like a lot, consider that there's about a twenty degree temperature difference between the rim and the Canyon floor.

Kaibab goes straight up and there's no water or shade. I reminded myself that it was better for me to run out of fluid than to preserve it.

I put myself in shutdown mode. No more looking around or wasting energy, just head down, no expression and forward movement. That's the way I did it when I ran in college. Every few steps I took a sip of water. I had a couple of Clif bars and pretzels for sodium.

Normally, a person can walk close to four miles an hour. My speed (if you want to call it that) would be less than two miles an hour, so I'd be climbing for over four hours. That was after descending for four hours. If you don't think it's a big deal to descend for that length of time, try it and see if you can walk the next day. But I've climbed Bright Angel in four and a half hours with fifty pounds strapped to my back and that was in the summer. That time, I camped overnight, so I hadn't completed all my hiking the same day. Also, there's no way to run out of water on Bright Angel because there's a tap at almost every mile marker.

I figured that my average step going up a hill was two feet long. If I took a drink of water every four steps and each drink was equivalent to one ounce of water and I had 124 ounces and the trail is 7.1 miles and there are 5,280 feet in a mile. I would be climbing 37,488 feet. 37,488 divided by eight is 4,686. So I would be over 4000 ounces of water short. Obviously, I would need to develop a new system. How about 16 ounces every mile, starting at the beginning of the first mile? 16 multiplied by 7 equals 112. Perfect.

I was about a mile up and I came across a family headed the other way. It was a mom and dad with two little girls.

"Hi. How's it going?" I asked.

"Good. It's just so beautiful," the dad replied.

"Where are you guys headed?" I asked. They weren't carrying backpacks so it didn't appear they were planning on camping.

"Just to the river. Then back up," the dad answered.

"Hope you know what you're in for? It's no stroll."

"Yes, we'll be fine."

"I'm not so worried about you. It's your daughters, I'm worried about," I replied.

"Look, I appreciate your concern, but we'll be fine."

No one can kick a dead horse like I can. Well, maybe Chuck. Yeah, what was I talking about? Chuck is the king of kicking a dead horse. Maybe I was channeling Chuck?

"People die down here. About a dozen a year. You better make sure your girls are getting enough water."

A concerned look came over the mom's face.

"Buddy. I don't appreciate you scaring my wife and kids. Why don't you get moving along?"

I let it go. I looked the wife in the eye and then at the daughters. It felt a little like I was at a funeral and saying goodbye to a friend. Maybe I made an impression? Maybe the mom would make sure her girls were drinking? Maybe she would talk her husband into camping at the Ranch? I had to let it go, though.

* * *

Not much happened on my ascent of South Kaibab. I wish I could weave some unbelievable story about a near death experience but my hike was pretty uneventful, except for one part. I probably ate too much and it was hot and I had to drink a great deal of liquid and had a lot of activity going on. My stomach started hurting about half way up. I did my best to ignore it and keep moving. I had about three miles to go when I really started to feel it. I thought it would be safe to let a little gas out but what came out wasn't gas. As soon as I realized my mistake, my butt cheeks clamped hard to stop the flow. I scrambled off the trail, past some brush and behind a large boulder. I unzipped my shorts and let them fall to the ground.

I needed to stabilize my polluted undergarments half way up my legs, while attempting to pull my oversized hiking boots through the leg holes of my shorts. I was almost free when I lost my balance and fell to the ground. If anyone had seen me with my shorts at my ankles and dirty drawers around my knees they might have thought I had been raped by a rogue mule. I had to rotate my body to a sitting position. Gravel and sand were pressed into my fecal sauce, creating a chunky dessert chili. I pulled off my shorts and then my offensive underpants. I threw those underneath the boulder that was hopefully sheltering me from any onlookers. Since I was surrounded by cactus, I had to use a medium sized rock to scrape the excess dirt from my inner ass.

I had to hike the rest of the way wearing the equivalent of sandpaper undershorts, and still needed to go. There might not be water on South Kaibab but fortunately there are bathrooms. I knew Cedar Ridge was one and half miles below the rim. Cedar Ridge is a popular destination for casual hikers. The only thing that can be more annoying than a long mule train are a bunch of happy, casual hikers. I must have looked like a deranged, feral hiker because the trail emptied as I approached the latrine. I was forced to wait my turn and then took far too long to complete my business. I saw nothing but disgusted looks when I exited the outhouse. I kept my head down and made my way back to the trail. My ass was an open wound. Every step felt like I was polishing the trauma with a sheet of sandpaper. The rest of the way, all I could think of was soaking in a soothing bath in my glorious hotel suite.

When I finally made it to the rim, I took about a second to congratulate myself and then hurried to the shuttle bus stop. My hike turned out to be more ass defying than death defying. I wanted to sit down on the bus, to rest my overworked legs but sitting wasn't an option. After a few stops I was back at El Tovar. I hobbled off the bus and up to the entrance of the hotel. I made it through the doors and just then Alexis appeared. I couldn't have looked or smelled worse. I had removed my hat on the shuttle and my hair must have looked like a pile of stained toothpicks swept together with a broom. If Alexis was attracted to me before, she might not be now.

"What happened to you?"

"I just got back from hiking to the bottom of the Canyon and back."

"You really smell."

No more acting cool.

"Want to have dinner tonight?"

"Are you going to shower beforehand?"

CHAPTER 24

―◁○▷―

I WENT STRAIGHT TO MY ROOM AND began a major fall cleaning. I took a bath and then a shower and used twice the amount of deodorant as I normally would have. My ass was in sorry shape. I had to spread Vaseline all around my hole so it wouldn't hurt as much when I walked.

I made myself a coffee and sat in my room's easy chair and tried not to move. It hurt when I first sat down but as long as I didn't adjust myself I was okay. You'd be amazed how many times you want to adjust your seating, though, like how many times you need to swallow when you have a sore throat.

I was supposed to meet Alexis at the El Tovar, Dining Room and Lounge at seven.

It's almost impossible to not include the "the" before "El". I guess you really can't mix languages unless it's French and English. French words and phrases seem to be the only words that come through un-interpreted (not sure that's a word). You have "cul de sac", "laissez-faire", "a la cart", "passé" and "soup du jour" to name just a few. Not sure what makes the French so special.

At six-forty-five I dragged my tired, douloureux fesses down to the restaurant. If I wasn't meeting Alexis for dinner, I would have ordered room service and passed out in my bed.

I asked for a table for two in the back of the restaurant and ordered a bottle of wine. Alexis arrived just after the wine and looked happy to see me.

As soon as I laid eyes on her the fatigue left my body and I forgot about my lacerated posterior. She had the nicest smile and the cutest voice. She was fine with me ordering the wine ahead of time.

She looked and smelled amazing. It was the same scent as before. It made me want to hold her down and bury my nose in her neck. I didn't think that would be a good idea. She was wearing a soft looking, green sweater with jeans. I hadn't noticed her figure before. She'd be good to have around if you needed to keep track of time. She was very feminine looking without being too made up. She was so sexy that I had to work to take my mind off of sex. It would be easy to slip up and be too forward. I had to keep it cool, so I fidgeted on my chair to make my ass hurt.

"How has your stay been?" I didn't know what to say and just wanted to say something. I tried to make my voice sound deeper because I figured she'd like that.

Alexis didn't punish me for my run of the mill question. "It's been fun. The kids were a lot to deal with. So afraid one might go over the edge."

"I can imagine." I was batting a thousand in bland conversation. "Is this the first time you've ever been to the Canyon?"

"Yes. It's amazing, isn't it?"

"The first time you see it, you can hardly believe it," I replied.

"If you go to the very first parking lot after you turn left off of the main road leading into the park; park there and sit near where the sidewalk from the parking lot intersects with the rim path. That's right about where a lot of people see the Canyon for the first time. It's pretty cool to watch everyone's reaction."

"Interesting. I might have to do that. It sounds fun. What about you? Have you been before?"

"I've been here a few times. The first time I came with my mom and sister. I spent a semester at the University of Arizona, in Tucson. They picked me up after the semester was over and we drove up."

"Where did they come from? I thought you said you were from Philadelphia?"

"Exactly. My mom and sister drove all the way from Philadelphia to pick me up from college. I guess my family can be a little strange. They wanted to see Arizona and my mom had a friend in Santa Fe."

"Oh, my, that's funny," Alexis exclaimed.

"Her friend used to send us her old Arizona Highways magazines. Which makes no sense because you'd figure it would have been a lot easier to buy my mom a subscription and her friend lived in New Mexico, not Arizona. I loved the magazine... I mean, it made Arizona seem like paradise."

"I've never seen the magazine but Arizona is a pretty amazing state. So diverse."

"Exactly. They only sell the magazine in Arizona. You can find it in the supermarket, near the checkouts. Funny because you're already there."

"Well go on with your story. I'm interested to hear about your first experience here."

"They drove to Tucson in a small hatchback. I had to get in the back with all my junk from school. My sister and I tied our camping gear to the roof of the car. We used a tarp to protect everything. We didn't make it to Phoenix before the tarp started coming undone. We had to move everything inside the car. I could hardly move in the backseat. My sister and I got into a fight because I left the used tarp under an overpass. My sister can be a bit much with stuff like that. She thought we were littering. I didn't feel like adding a dirty, disgusting tarp to everything else I had going on in the back of the car."

"Ah, family life."

"Right? Well, we drove straight through Phoenix. We stopped at some caverns, I forget the name. They told us that we would think the tour was shorter than it was because we'd be so far underground. They were right. I thought they moved the clocks ahead when we were down in the cave.

"We didn't have a lot of money so we sort of skimped on hotels. We made it to the Canyon the same day. We were lucky because our campsite, whoever had it before must have been some kind of camping expert."

"What do you mean?"

"They had made a bed of pine needles and then placed their tent on top of that. We did the same and it turned out to be quite comfortable. It was me, my mom and sister all sharing the same tent. It was June but it's over six thousand feet on the South Rim so it can get pretty chilly at night. One night, it got very cold and I had to spoon my mom. ...I'm still dealing with that memory."

"I bet. Oh jeez, look at the time. I have to catch a flight in the morning..." Alexis had me going and then smiled.

"My psychologist warned me not to repeat that story."

"That's pretty good advice."

"Anyway. We all survived the night. The next morning I got into a terrible fight with my sister. I can't even remember what about. I walked to the rim alone. I met a girl that worked in the village. I was ready to get a job and stay here. I would have been our waiter tonight.

"If I was Tony Bennett I would have written that song about the Canyon but the lyrics wouldn't have flowed, which is probably why I'm not Tony Bennett."

"I'll say."

"We left that same day. We drove straight to Santa Fe, to see my mom's friend. I think we spent a night there and then drove the rest of the way back to Pennsylvania, nonstop. Normally, you'd spend two nights sleeping in hotels in that distance. I remember waking up in the front seat and seeing my mom in some sort of driving coma, going eighty. She never drove over sixty-five! I can't believe we made it back alive."

"So your family hadn't heard of air travel?"

"Funny. My dad lost his job so we had to make do. My mom was already pretty frugal. The first time I ever flew in a plane was in college. But let me continue."

"It's such a long story," Alexis commented, then smiled.

"So we drove like thirty six hours straight, something like that. When I was at college, I worked in the kitchen, washing dishes. One of my coworkers was this pretty Asian girl, from Japan. I think she said she wanted to see the East Coast. I was like, 'Well if you're ever in Philadelphia...' We arrived home, finally. My mom was half crazy at that point because she did the bulk of the driving. We walked in the house and that girl was there. My dad was pronouncing her name like he was Japanese. My mom was so annoyed. She sort of hated the Japanese too, because she carpooled with a Chinese woman for close to twenty years."

"Oh my god! Your poor mother."

"Yeah, my dad could get a little creepy around women.

"I had to take the girl on a tour downtown the next day. I think because of all the driving and I'd done a shit load of drinking in Tucson... The next day, we were at the pier, you know, on the Delaware River? I was with this girl and..." I caught myself. "You know, I survived the spooning story... I might be pushing it."

"You have to tell me now. You did something with the Asian girl?"

"No! Never even crossed my mind, actually. I've thought about that since. I mean she was cute and everything. I guess I shared my mom's disgust and didn't want to potentially follow my father."

"Okay, I don't know your dad but that's gross."

"Yeah, sorry. What happened is probably worse. Jeez, not sure why I'm telling you this. It's like I got going with this super long story and now I am like a runaway train."

"Just tell me. You'll probably never see me again," Alexis said with a smile.

"Okay... I crapped my pants."

Alexis choked on her food and bust out laughing. "Wow! So gross."

"I can't believe I just told you that. It's like you put truth serum in my wine."

"Now I know why you're here alone."

"Yeah, no kidding."

"I peed myself once," Alexis offered.

"What?!" I replied laughing.

"When I was a girl, I had this stupid crush on Tom Selleck of all people."

"Man, you have daddy issues."

"Possibly. Well, I was backstage, down in the bowels of the theater we were playing in. I was concentrating on the pending performance," Alexis took a break, bit into a roll and fanned her face with her hand. "I took a blind corner and ran smack into Tom Selleck! I was so surprised, I wet myself. I mean, we were standing three inches apart and you could hear water dripping onto the floor."

We both burst out laughing.

"Wait, that's crazy but 'backstage'? What do you mean?"

"It was a U2 concert. I'm a backup singer."

"No way! That's cool." Alexis just got even better looking. "Really?"

"Yeah. It's really no big deal. I've toured with U2, Luther Vandross, The Stones… I guess when I start naming the acts it does sound like a big deal."

"Wow. I'm impressed. I've always been a big fan of music."

"Wow, way to go out on a limb," Alexis shot back. "Sorry. I shouldn't do that. My sister tells me that's why I'm still single," Alexis confessed.

"I don't mind. You sound like my friends. They're all guys, though. Guess you should tone it down a bit. But that backup singer thing, that's cool. I always thought it was 'background' singer?"

"No, it's 'backup' or 'backing vocalist'."

"Oh. I like 'backing vocalist'. Is it okay if I call you that? I won't even use your first name anymore."

"Actually, I would prefer that. That's what Bowie did. 'Hey you, backing vocalist' Alexis said with this horrible, phony English accent.

227

"Now you're just name dropping."

"Ah, from music royalty to having dinner with an incontinent loner. How I have fallen," Alexis lamented. "What was up with you today? You looked horrible."

"Well, I mean, I hiked close to twenty miles…"

"But you were like, 'Want to have dinner?' and then you high-tailed it out of there."

"I wasn't really looking my best. You know, with my hat head and all."

"No you weren't, but you were walking funny too."

"I was really tired."

"It was a different kind of walk."

"What, are you an investigator?"

"Just that you have this pants shitting history…"

"Are you asking me if I crapped my pants again today?"

"Maybe," Alexis smiled, leading me on.

I took a little too long to reply.

"Oh, my fucking God! I was just messing with you! You got a real problem, don't you?"

"I think it was the heat and all the effort…"

"It's always something with you. Is that how you stay so thin?"

"Yeah, maybe that's it. I shit everything I eat. Oh wait, doesn't everyone do that?"

"I make myself throw up. That's why I'm always chewing gum."

"And thank you for that."

You know how I knew Alexis was the one? I ended up telling her the whole shart story and she laughed so hard she almost reenacted her Tom Selleck story. She even asked to see my shredded bum.

The crazy thing is I didn't have a problem showing it to her or letting her attend to it. I didn't feel uncomfortable or self-conscious. Afterwards, I asked her if she had any areas that needed attention. As you can tell I can be quite the smooth operator.

Alexis ended up spending the night and I woke up the next morning and felt more relaxed than I'd felt in years. I wasn't in a hurry to get out of bed or go anywhere.

"So what's your story?" Alexis asked as she looked around the room.

"What do you mean?"

"This is quite the room."

"I got a deal online."

"Yeah right. You're like some rich, loner dude. Maybe you *are* an embezzler!"

"Maybe."

"It's weird that I didn't ask you that yet. I feel like such a whore."

"We were too busy discussing my problem. Besides, you'd only be a whore if I paid you."

"Okay. Whew! I was worried there, Alexis sighed. "So, what about it?'

"I was a network engineer and then helped design and develop an internet dating site. I'm in between jobs. Not sure what I'm going to do next. I sort of like not working."

"It makes me a little uneasy. If I go two-weeks between gigs I can get a little stir crazy."

"That's probably a good thing."

"Well that dating site must have been a real hit. Which one? I'm on half a dozen."

"MovieDate."

"That was you?! And you thought it was a big deal that I was a backing vocalist."

She was impressed. Even better that she had already been so before she knew anything about my success.

"I have backing vocalust," I said, raising and lowering my eyebrows.

"That was so bad," Alexis replied.

"What's your sister and the kids up to today?"

"She left with them yesterday. I didn't want to tell you before. Wanted you to think that someone would be looking for me in the morning."

"I see, but now I know you're here alone."

"I text messaged my sister your room number when you were in the bathroom. Say, I didn't think you used the bathroom?" Alexis said with a puzzled look on her face.

"Very funny. How were you planning on getting home?"

"Wasn't sure. I guess I figured, I'd either rent a car or take the train. Wasn't too worried about it."

My kind of woman.

"I really shouldn't be left alone, the shape my bottom is in. I think it would be wise if we stayed together, at least for the next few days."

Alexis smiled. "You're probably right. And now, you're sort of my responsibility since I attended to you and everything."

With that I had a traveling partner. I had left Philadelphia ten days prior, alone and without much thought of the future. Ten days later I was with a woman I didn't ever want to be away from. Funny how things can work out.

EPILOGUE

JOHN, EDDIE AND CHUCK NEVER CASHED the checks I gave them.

Eddie wrote "void" on his check so he wouldn't be tempted. He said he didn't need my money, that he was doing fine with his telecom agency. I did enough for him already, he added, helping him close the theater chain deals.

John told me thanks but no thanks. "The CWA took care of me, thank you very much."

The CWA was the Communication Workers of America, the union that supported employees of the phone company.

I guess Chuck was worth more than I estimated. He did a nice job investing the buyout he received from the phone company and kept his expenses to a minimum. He still lives in the house near the railroad tracks.

If Chuck and Britt needed something, like a new couch or bed, with her eyebrows raised, Britt would ask, "Should I go get the check?" Then there would be silence. "No?" More silence. "Ookaay," Britt would pout.

* * *

Chuck's Grandma died. I was worried that Chuck would be devastated but he's actually taking it pretty well. He figures that she missed Chuck's Grandfather and now they're together in heaven. I know Chuck's grandfather had some issues but Chuck assures me that his Grandma got his Grandpa in.

We decided to watch Monday Night Football at Dawson's. Chuck's Grandma's memorial took place a couple weeks ago. Chuck was one of the speakers.

"I'm not happy with my eulogy."

"What do you mean? I thought it was great."

"I was afraid to recite it from memory; that's why I read it but then cousin Timmy went up and did his off the cuff and I think more people appreciated his."

"It wasn't a competition."

"Still. How many times am I going to have an audience like that?"

"There's something very wrong with you. What did you want to say?"

"I've been thinking about it quite a bit."

"Really? You?"

"Yes. Want me to do take a stab at it?"

"Go ahead."

"I would have said: This probably isn't the best thing to say in church, but IF there is a heaven, my Grandma is there right now. I mean, she pretty much lived a perfect life. Her one sin was that she said some things about certain people and that was it. One sentence, that's it.

"My Grandma had five older siblings and none of them attended college. Her parents didn't attend. No one in her family knew anything about college. No one in her family expected her to go, but she figured it out. She went to Catholic University in D.C. She was in the capital when there were still 'whites only' drinking fountains. My Grandma made a point out of drinking from the 'colored' fountains.

"Grandma had six kids and didn't work for more than ten years but when Grandpa lost his job she went back to work to save the family. Grandma's first job was the midnight to eight shift at a nearby nursing home. From there, she retired as a nursing school instructor.

"My Grandma got up before six and didn't take a break until she took a bath and sat down with a glass of beer. In between she worked, cleaned the house, did the laundry, including washing and ironing Grandpa's hankies.

"Villanova let people sixty-five and over attend college for free. They did that because they assumed no one over sixty-five would be interested. Well, they didn't know my Grandma. She took a physics course because Grandpa was a physicist and she wanted to understand the subject better. I feel sorry for the college kids in my Grandma's classes because she wouldn't be the one looking at the clock, hoping class would soon be over; I'm sure she asked questions right up to the very end of class.

"Getting back to heaven. IF there is a heaven, Grandma's there now. And it wouldn't be heaven to Grandma without Grandpa, so he's there too. Grandma's list of sins is one sentence long; Grandpa's is over a page. I'm sure the other people in heaven are asking each other how HE got in."

The last part made me smile. Chuck and I sat quiet for a minute or two. I took a sip of my beer and wondered if Chuck's Grandma was doing the same.